I0710462

THE ORIGIN

THE FIVE

BRUCE E. SCOTT

Copyright © 2024 by Bruce E. Scott.

ISBN 978-1-962587-17-4 (softcover)
ISBN 978-1-962587-18-1 (ebook)

All rights reserved. No part of this book may be reproduced or transmitted in any form or by any means, electronic or mechanical, including photocopying, recording, or by any information storage and retrieval system without express written permission from the author, except in the case of brief quotations embodied in critical reviews and certain other noncommercial uses permitted by copyright law.

This book is a work of fiction. Names, characters, places, and incidents are the product of the author's imagination or are used fictitiously. Any resemblance to actual locales, events, or persons, living or dead, is purely coincidental.

Printed in the United States of America.

INTRODUCTION

In book two William Bradford is dead, everybody is celebrating their freedom from slavery, from the plantation, and from the town. William Bradford's children are happy for the first time not being under his control anymore, and one of them even found love with John one of The Five.

On the third night of the celebrating, The Five and lots of people are sitting around one of the many campfires that was burning outside of town under the night stars, they were asked to tell their story on how this all got started.

Book two tells how each of The Five reveals how they begin.

ACKNOWLEDGMENT

First, I thank the Lord Thy God, in using me as a vessel to write about The Five. Thanks to my fiancé Sylvia for her support, also my new fans in pushing me to produce The Five second book.

CONTENTS

Scott's Story

SCOTT'S TABLE OF CONTENTS

C H A P T E R   1

Celebration

**The celebration has been going on for three days
and there are no signs of stopping.**

On the third night, everyone settled down around a large campfire telling jokes, stories and bragging on what took place at William Bradford's plantation, while enjoying tasty food and drinks. The campfire gives a romantic glow in the night. The sky is clear, the stars are so bright it would appear you could reach up and touch them.

Wanda, one of the people Sylvia trained, looks at Scott and takes the opportunity to ask a question that she had always wanted to ask, for a long time.

"Tell me Scott how did your city came to be?" Said Wanda.

Scott took another drink of his ale; then he took a cloth and wiped his mouth. He looked at Wanda and said, "Well Wanda, to make this interesting and more believable I thank each of us should tell their own part of the story. I will go first."

He took a deep breath and said, "The story goes like this."

I was a young child that was raised by two of the kindest parents that a child could hope for. My mother's name is Gertrude Martin who stood about 5 ft. 7 in, long blond hair that came just below her shoulders, she was always busy, taken care of me, my father, the house, cooking and cleaning, talking with the neighbor's weather if it is at their house, or ours.

My father's name is Simon Martin a well build man, with a full head of black hair. He was a strong, but gentle man, and very smart, we owned a few businesses in our growing town called Yellow River.

I was the type of boy that always wanted to know more. always willing to learn as much as I can about the history of this country. I also wanted to know why our people settled here and how our laws govern our way of life.

The things I learn not only from school, but life itself, and what can help me achieve goals I set for myself, I must admit at that time my goals were different back then. I just wanted to learn the family business, but God had something else plan for me. My mother always told me to treat people the same as you wanted to be treated. I took that to heart.

I did a lot of exploring when I was a young man, and wonder further, and further away from home each day, and when I came back, I told my mother and father what I have learn and seen. Most of the time my father already knew what I seen but never discouraged me.

Long before I started my exploration my father took me out for a few days to teach me how to live off the land. He showed me how to trap rabbits, squirrels, and how-to fish. He did not know much, and most of the time he was guesting, however, it was enough to keep me alive. During the time I was gone I discovered signs of the natives that live in the area. To me this was exciting, I heard about the Indians that live here, but never seen them. I was told that they could be dangerous. So, when I saw the native at a distance. I kept it hidden because I did not know what to expect.

When I came back home, I told my parents about the Indians I have seen.

My mother became worried, she said, "You shouldn't go that far away from home."

My mother was a loving woman that care about her family.

Simon said, "the next time I go out I should be armed."

My Father took me out of town and taught me how to use a musket and pistol. That is when I learn that my father was very skill with weapons. I did not leave again until I was as good as him. During this time after we have done some target practice, we would sit down under a huge oak tree and talk. He told me of a great Ocean off the west coast of this country.

Simon said, "I have never seen it, I only heard talks of it, and the wonders beyond the other side of the ocean. He heard talk about wonders unlike any other place in the world."

It was a lot to take in. I decided, I had to see this ocean and. The wonders my father spoke of.

So, after a long talk with my parents about what I am planning on during. We prayed for my safety, and a safe return. I pack my backpack, kiss my mother, with tears in her eyes she said, I love you my son, please take care of yourself. and with my father we walked out of the house.

My father walks me to the edge of town going over everything he taught me, he said, "The skills I taught you are to defend yourself. Not to start trouble."

I told him, "I understood."

He told me, "I am proud of you Scott when you ready come back to us.

We hugged each other, and I sat off headed west. I did not know that would be the last time I would see them alive.

I started my way west to see the wonders my father told me about, but I never made it there until years later.

A week has passed, and I am still headed West. I made camp near some woods, and I just got through chopping wood for my fire, I have placed my hatchet down, when an Indian came running in my camp. He was about 5 ft 8 in. tall, and very fit, he had long black hair, which was wet from his sweat. He was running away from something or someone.

You could tell by how hard he was breathing he must have been running for a long time.

When he saw me, we were surprised, and we froze looking at each other? I never seen an Indian up close before.

It was not long when that someone he was running from came running into my camp on foot. It was two men chasing the Indian. Where they came from, I could not tell you.

Just for a moment the Indian though I was with the two men, you could see he was worried and scared. All of that was about to change.

Both men were short and dirty, one was thin, the other overweight and breathing hard, so hard he knelt to rest after the run.

I had to ask, "hey sir, are you going to make it?"

The thin man spoke for his fat friend, "shut up."

Their teeth are stained with tobacco and were missing two in the front and two on the left side of his mouth.

The fat man was still trying to catch his breath, so the thin man spoke again.

"Who are you and what are you doing with our Ingin?"

"Your what?" Replied Scott.

"Our Ingin?" Said the man again.

"What is an Ingin?" I ask.

"Our Ingin." The thin man said again this time louder as he was pointing at the Indian.

"OOOOO, you mean Indian." said Scott.

"Yes. That is what my friend said." said the fat man still have not recover fully.

Scott said calmly, "Well your Ingin went that way." Pointed in the opposite direction from the way they came. Me and my Indian friend here, just started to sit down to have something to eat. You must be in a hurry to catch up to your Ingin, of course he has put distance from you by now. But you should be able to catch up to him with no problem."

The fat man said, "I thank he is making fun of us?"

The thin man said, "Is that right boy? Are you making fun of us?"

Scott answered, "No sir. I thank you are doing that all by yourself." The fat man told his friend, "He is making fun of us. Let us kill him and take his Ingen."

When the thin man told his friend that, I look at my new friend. The Indian cult my eyes, I look down toward the hatchet. The Indian follow my eyes and saw my foot slide under the hatchet, he understands what I was about to do.

Scott said, "kill? That is a hard word. Will you men reconsider and go after your own Ingin.

Just then the two men step toward us. That is when I flip my hatchet to my new-found friend, then I drew my knife.

We made short work of the two men and kill them bout. My Indian friend took on the thin man, and I had the fat man, still weak from his run he wildly swung his knife at my Chest, and at the same time he stumbles, I step forward buried my knife in the side of his neck, and that in the first time I kill someone. I turned to see how my friend was doing. He had just pulled my hatch out of the thin man chest.

After we have triumph over the two men, we look at each other smiling. I noticed my friend's smile went away and in its place was concern. He pointed at my chest. When I looked down and saw my blood, suddenly I became weak, I had been cut deep across my chest. I fell to my knees and passed out.

A Strange World

When I woke up, I had no idea how long I had been unconscious, where I was, how I got here, and what my condition was a mystery. All I knew that a woman was leaning over me, taken care of my worn. Her face was smooth, her hair had two braids, one on each side of her head.

When she saw my eyes open. She stood up and left in a hurry. I followed her with my eyes as she ran out. She stood about 5ft. 7in. I try to stand up and follow her. Suddenly pain went through my chest, and I remembered that I had been wounded. Pain has a way of bringing that back into your mind.

I also realized I did not have any clothes on. I looked around for my clothes but the only thing I saw was my pants.

I struggle to put them on. My chest was throbbing, my head was cloudy, and it was hard to keep my balance. I had to see where I was. So, I fault through the pain. Twice I fell, the second time I failed I just sat there and put my pants on one leg, and then the other. again, I struggled to get to my feet, this time I was more determined.

When I became stable, I pulled up my pants, went to the open of the tent and stepped into another world. I. WAS. LOST. And I had no idea where I was.

I was in an Indian Village. Where I was, I did not know. I did not know if I was a prisoner or a guest.

I just stood there outside of the tent; my mind was not only cloudy but confused. Everyone who noticed me stopped what they were doing and just stared at me. Now I am scared. I could not move, until the women that was in the tent with me came back. She took me by the hand and led me to another tent.

This tent was big, I mean BIG! She pulls open the flap to the big tent and jesters me to go inside. I just stood there looking at her. She kelp trying to get me to enter it.

I look around and saw a few Indian men who was just standing around the tent smiling. They too, jester me to go in.

For some unknow reason I felt a little less nervous. I looked at the tent for a few moments and I went inside.

The first person I saw was the man I fault beside. We smile at each other and nod our heads slightly.

Then something shook me to my gut. He spoke to me in English. He said, "Please sit down."

Once I sat down, he introduced himself, "my name is Bear Claw, you are in my Father's Village, our tribe is known as the Black Foot. My father is the Chief. His name is Chief Mingan."

His father stared right though me, without blinking, he stood about 5 ft. 6 inches tall, and his face was hard looking.

Before I sat down. I look around, there was seven other men. Three older men and four middle-aged men.

As I was sitting down, I took in the layout of the inside of the tent. There were a lot of blankets on the floor, which covered the entire floor except in the middle. In the middle of the tent there was a circle of stones, inside the circle was wood that had been burning but now it was just glowing.

At the head, Bear Claw's Father sat. I tried my best to remain calm. Chief Mingan spoke in his native tongue. Bear Claw translated.

"Thank you for saving my son's life, Bear Claw told me what happen."

Scott said, "I do not know about that. It looks like your son saved me. I pointed at my chest. It is I who should thank him, and you for haven my wounds look after."

"Why are you out here all alone?" Said Chief Mingan.

"Before I answer your question allow me to introduce myself. My name is Scott Martin, I left home to seek knowledge, to learn more about this land I live in. To better myself," Bear Claw translated what I said.

"And what do you thank you can learn from us?" Chief Mingan wanted to know.

"Well from what I have seen since I been with Bear Claw, I saw how he fights without getting hurt." Said Scott.

After Bear Claw translated what I said, everyone laughed aloud. This put me at ease for the first time since I opened my eyes.

I continued from there.

"I would like to see what this land has to offer, I like to learn how to heal wombs, like the one I received, I would like to know how you achieved harmony in your village. Your people look strong, how do you feed so many people? I also like to learn how you hunt."

Bear Claw translated.

Chief Mingan said, "Is there anything else, maybe how to bath or how to pee?" Everyone again laughed.

Bear Claw translated.

I smile and say, "No thank you there are somethings I can do on my own." Said Scott.

Everyone laughed again but not as loud.

The Chief called Bear Claw over to him and said something in his ear. What he said made Bear Claw get up and walk toward me. Bear Claw said, "come with me."

I got up and bowed to the Chief because I did not know what else to do, or the proper way of leaving the Chief and his Council. I went to Bear Claw and ask,

"Did I say something wrong?" Ask Scott.

Bear Claw replied, "No you did not, you have shown honor, and respect to my father and the council. They told me to teach you all you ask for. This is for saving my life."

I stop Bear Claw, and look him in his eyes and said, "Thank you for saving mine."

Bear Claw did not respond until we arrived back at the tent I was in when I woke up.

"We will start your training after your wound heal."

Two weeks later my training began. My wounds healed enough to start, I felt like I had never been hurt. Now I am ready to start training.

As the weeks passed Bear Claw taught me a lot. First, how to ride a horse in the beginning. I was just trying not to fall off, however later I became exceptionally good at it.

He did what his father told him to do. He taught me everything I asked for and then some. My training went on for days. Then days turn into weeks, and weeks turn into months.

One day we went on a hunting trip, we did not catch much, just a few rabbits. The hunting trip took us far away from the village. Bear Claw and I decided to make camp where we were, we skin, and gutted the rabbits then prepare to eat.

The night was cool, but the fire was warm, the stars were bright in the sky. The sounds of the night echoing cricket. and coyotes howling in the distance, it was very pleasant.

I ask Bear Claw, "Where did you learn how to speak English?"

Curiously, Bear Claw ask, "What is English?"

Scott smile and said, "English is the words you use to speck with me." That is when Bear Claw told me his story.

CHAPTER 3

The Circus

Bear Claw started his story by saying, "Like you I wanted to see if there is more to life than my village, so with my father good wishes I went into the unknown and followed the sun set. The first two or three days there was nothing to do, I ate off the land, did some fishing and kept going, in the morning I had the sun at my back and in the afternoon, I followed the sunset.

One day I came across some wagons with some strange people in them. A few of them painted their faces white, with a red smile, and a big red nose. Their feet and hands were huge, it was difficult for them to get around, but they managed. They had to raise their legs high, to walk. There was a man tall as trees, all he did was walk around.

There was a man who is extraordinarily strong, a fat woman and a skinny man, who was her mate.

They were all led by a man called the ringmaster, he wore a tall hat and carry a whip with him everywhere he went. The hat he wore was round, tall, and black.

At first it was hard for us to understand each other, so we used sign language. They taught me the white man language. After a while it was easy to understand what we were saying to each other. But that was not half of it. The animals that were traveling with them were very strange. I have never seen anything like them before.

There was one animal with a hump in its back, and it was always chewing. The ringmaster called this animal a camel, another was noticeably big, the biggest animal I have seen, the animals is called, an elephant, this animal had ears as big as the entrance way to my father tent, his nose was long as a horse's leg.

There was another animal whose neck is exceptionally long. It is called a giraffe.

There are animals that they kept in cage age; they were dangerous. These are the only animals I can compare them with the mountain lion, but these cats are much bigger, and look quite different, one cat had lots of hair around his head. He was called a loin. The other cat was yellow with black stripes or black with yellow stripes, he was called a Tiger.

These strange peoples called their tribe a circus, and they never had an Indian with them. They asked me to join their tribe. Well since they were going in the same direction that I was going, I decided to travel with them, during that time I learned more of the white man words, the sad moment came when we had to part ways. The Ringmaster gave me money for my performance. The money came in handy. I use it to buy things I need.

When I came home a big feast was given in my honor. I told my father what I learned. He was please, now we can talk to the white man. And when I told them what I saw. No one believed me, that animals are like that. It did not matter; I was back with my people.

The Ringmaster also told me a little about their religious belief.

He said, "The great spirit looks over us all, he looks over the grass, the trees, the animals, fish in the water, and the great Spirit made man Dominant over everything."

When we came back from our hunt, it was unsuccessful, we had a few rabbits and a deer or two. With the food we already have, and what we return with, it will last us for a few days.

Other than the food shortage everything else was going very well. I even fell in love with the most beautiful woman in the village, she had long black hire, her eyes seem to twinkle in the moonlight, her skin was smooth as water without wind, and it seem to glow. When she looked at me my heartbeat strongly. My love for her was overwhelming. Her name is Pita, she is Bear Claw sister, Chief Mingan daughter. Pita is the first woman I had ever met that I gave my heart to. She stood 5 ft. 9 in. which was tall for her people, and she received a lot of respect from the tribe, and binge Bear Claw sister, had a lot to do with that.

Even though some of the Braves were envious of me, everyone thought that we were a good match.

While the small talk was going around the village, two of our scouts galloped into the village yelling that they have seen buffalo close to here.

Excitement came over the village, and with that news everyone knew that the village would not go hungry this winter.

Me and the rest of the Braves gather our weapons to leave for the hunt. I have never seen a buffalo before so, this is new to me, Bear Claw said to me, "this will be a great hut." I notice most of the Braves are going on this hut.

During the time we was away, Pita, Koko, and the rest of the women from the village went into the woods to collect wood, to start a fire for cooking the Buffalo. Other women went with them to collect blades of grass, and water. The grass used to make baskets and bowls. The grass is about a foot and a half long, and an inch wide. Before Pita, and Koko filled their jugs with water, they decided to go for a swim against the advice of the other women.

"Come join us," said Pita.

"No, it is too dangerous, and you should come out. There is mountain man that lurks in these woods, it is unsafe."

Koko yielded, "go back to the village, we will join you there. The mountain man has not been seen in many moons."

The woman threw their arms in the air. In disgust, then turn left.

After a while Pita and Koko decided to go back to the village. "We better get back before the sun goes behind the mountains." said Pita.

CHAPTER 4

Trouble

Koko nodded in agreement. The two-woman splashed each other playfully on their way to the shore, both women climb out of the water naked, water dripping from their body. They collect their clothes and start to get dressed. That is when Koko began to have an eerie feeling that they were being watched. Both women look around. Pita told Koko that she saw someone standing among the trees. He was a big man watching them, and he was not even trying to hide.

Patti and Koko look at each other. They hurried to pick up the rest of their clothes and started to walk toward their village. At first the man that the woman seen just watch them as they walk away. After a few seconds he started to follow them, not trying to catch up with them, he just walked behind them. The woman starts to run, but only for a few steps. They came to a sudden stop. In front of them was another man. He just stood there. The woman looks behind them and the man behind them kept coming. The woman looks to their left and there was a third man. Panic started to sit in on both women. Without thanking the woman began to run to their right this time their path was clear. No one that they could see was in front of them. Pita and Koko ran for a long time until. Pita fell, exhausted from the run. Koko tried to help her up, but Pita was too tired.

"Keep moving," Koko said.

Pita could not stand up. Koko tried again to help Pita up.

"Get up," said Koko.

"I can't run Koko, go, get away." Pita said.

In Koko effort in trying to get Pita up and running again, one of the men caught up with them. He knocks Koko to the ground and jumps on top of her. Koko tried to defend herself, but the man was too strong. The man is large and dirty, with dirty hair, bad breath and a few front teeth missing. He pinned Koko to the ground and laughed.

The man said, "You are mine now."

After he said that a big grin came down his face.

Just then Pita struggle to her feet pick up a rock and hit the man in the head. It knocks him off Koko, but it did not render him unconcise, but it was enough to free Koko.

Pita is now having her second wind. The women started to run again, but to no avail.

The other two men caught up with the women. This time bought women was overwhelmed. The women were beaten badly especially Pita. The man that beat her was the same man Pita hit on the head.

The mountain men drag Pita and Koko back to their camp which was a cave halfway up the mountain.

When they reach their camp, they beat the women some more, and rape them.

After the men took turn on each of the women, the men tied the women hand and feet. When the women were secure back in the cave. They sat around their campfire eating ribbits and drinking whiskey, talking, and laughing about what just took place. They were pleased and felt good.

They will soon regret everything.

They drink a lot and soon fall into a deep drunken sleep.

In the cave Pita and Koko are in unbearable pain, but still, they struggle with their bonds.

It was Koko who untied herself, then aided Pita with her restraints.

Koko ask Pita, "can you walk?"

Pita answer with a nod and said, "yes."

The two women gather themselves and very quietly slip pass their captives and down the mountain. They stumbled through the woods naked, every step was very painful, it seemed like hours, soon they came upon the pond where all of this started. Koko and Pita fell unconscious, neither had the strength to go any further.

The women from the village were worried, Koko and Pita have not return yet. The Villager's form a search party and went to look for their sister.

It did not take long for the search party to find the two women; they started their search at the pond because that is where Koko and Pita were last seen.

They found Koko and Pita at the pound unconscious, and barely breathing. They did their best in trying to get the two women back to their Village, but doing the short journey both women pass-a-way.

Before Koko pass, she manages to say two words, "Mountain men."

The hunt went well, the hunting party kill a lot of Buffalo, but only enough of what they needed to feed the village for the winter. They used the Buffalo skin to keep themselves warm.

Everyone at the party was feeling good. They loaded up the meat and fur and headed back to the Village unaware of what took place there.

As we got closer to the village, I began to get a very uneasy feeling that I had never felt before. I was really concerned I could not tell you what it was but, the closer we got, the worse it became. I looked at Bear Claw and his facial expression, and body language was telling me he has the same feeling. It was so strong that when we got insight of the village, Bear Claw raised his hand to stop the hunting party. We all stayed settled on our horses and just stared at the village trying to see what was wrong. One of the braves left behind to protect the village saw us and ran toward us.

Bear Claw and I move forward to meet him.

The brave told us, "Koko, and Pita are dead."

The news hit us both hard, I wanted to throw up. I felt sick to my stomach, but I quickly snapped out of it, Bear Claw and I set out toward the village in a full Gallup.

Bear Claw arrived at his tent first, he jumped off his horse before it came to a stop. I was close being him and was followed by the rest of the hunting party. Bear Claw ran into his tent and saw Pita and Koko wrapped in a white cloth. He fell to his knees and just stared at his wife and sister's corpse.

I do not know what went through his mind, but I can tell you what went through mine. Hate and revenge, how can someone do this to two of God's angels. Bear Claw felt the same way. These men need to die and die slowly.

Chief Mingan summoned Bear Claw and me to his tent, Mingan gestured for us to sit down.

The Chief said, "Koko and Pita were beaten and rape. You two are to find these men and bring them back to the village alive. This will give our people justice, and make sure you bring back the right men."

Bear Claw and I said nothing, we just stood up and walked out of the tent. We did not agree what Mingan side, but we will obey him.

Mingan followed us out of the tent knowing what he said would be obeyed.

We mounted our horses. Bear Claw looked at his father and said, "We will be back before the burial ceremony."

Mingan nodded his head. Then we rode off to find Koko and Pita murderous.

At the end of the village on horseback was the hunting party. The Buffalo meat and skin was secure in the village, and they were waiting to join us.

We did not stop or slow down, we road passed them not saying anything, they just fell in behind us.

In my head I was trying to form a plan to take these men alive, which was hard to do because, my mine clouded with hate, I could hardly think.

We stop two hundred yards from the Mountain where the murderous lives. Halfway up we could see the entrance of the cave where Koko and Pita were kept. We join the young braves Chief Mingan sent ahead to keep an eye on those men.

Bear Claw, me, and all the worries except two went up the side of the Mountain on foot. The two stayed behind to watch the horses.

The cave was high on the Mountain, but the trail made it easy to get there. As we got closer to the mouth, we noticed there were two guards sitting and talking. They did not see us coming until it was too late.

We all positioned ourselves around their camp and waited for Bear Claw signal.

Bear Claw gave the signal to advance. He signals two of the braves to rush the two guards and with the side of their ax hits them on their head knocking them unconscious. What went through my mind was what Mingan said, have proof and bring them back alive. We enter the cave and saw the other two men in a drunken sleep. Before we made our presence known, two of the braves found Koko and Pita clothes.

That is when Bear Claw kicked one of the men. He woke up startled, this woke up his friend, they laid there, eyes wide open and on us. One of the men reach for his knife. I jumped on him with my knife drawn and begged him.

"Please, please, give me an excuse to cut your throat."

The man relaxes. We bind their hands and push them down the Mountain. Some of the worriers pick up Koko and Pita clothes and everyone regroups at the horses. As we walk to our horse one of the Mountain men said to me. "You are a white man, one of us, you won't let them harm us, will you?"

This filled me with rage, I slowly turn to face the man, he was smiling and nod his head as if I were going to agree with him. I could not control myself. I hit that man hard in the face he went down at the might of my blow. I jump on top of the man and hit him again in his face repeatedly.

At first Bear Claw and the Braves just watched, but then I would not stop. Bear Claw grab me and remind me what his father said, "Bring them back alive." said Bear Claw.

A rope was tied to their bonded hands, and the other end to my horse. Bear Claw had the other man tide to his horse.

We started back to the village at a light Gallup, at first the men ran a long with us then they fell, and we drag them the rest of the way back to the village. The Chief said bring them back alive. He did not say what shape they had to be in.

After a brief convention with Mingan and the counselor, Bear Claw emerged from the tent. He instructed his Braves to put the two men on their back, stretch their arms over their heads, and tied their hands to a steak. Then he orders their legs apart and tied their ankles to a steak, after that he told his braves to make a small fire between their legs close to their, technical so they will die a slow, and painful death.

My plans were to stay with Pita and the Black Foot tribe for the rest of my life, but now everything has changed. The only thing I could think of is home.

I stayed with Bear Claw and his people for another year until I got over Pita and was able to move on.

I had a lot of hate for those Mountain man.

I never look at another Black Foot woman after Pita again.

One day, some braves and I went on a hunt for Buffalo. That is when I saw three wagons headed West. This was my chance to learn about what was happening back East.

This is the first white people I have seen since the Mountain Man.

When we approach them, you can see the fear coming over their faces. The women and children jumped in the wagon out of fear; the men grabbed their weapons.

We stopped our approach. I told the Braves that I will go in alone.

It was not until I spoke English to them when they became a little at ease.

Scott said, "Where did you come from, and how are things back East?"

A tall thin man about five feet ten inches. Black hair and a thin mustache are the leader. His name is Ben.

Ben and I talked for a while, after he had his party, made camp early and invited us all to dinner, all of us including the Braves. We accept, the women fix dinner for us that remind me of my mother's cooking.

Ben and I sat down and talked about what's happening back East. He told me that war was going to happen. Everyone is talking about it.

Ben said, "a group of us do not want anything to do with war, so we decide to head West."

We all talk a little longer, Then I thank Ben for his hospitality, and the haunting party and went back to the village.

I told Bear Claw. "I must leave to see about my parents back home."

Bear Claw said, "it is good to have known you." He agrees and understands what I said and why.

The next day I said my goodbyes to Chief Mingan and the rest of the Braves and headed East.

Because of the special bond we have, Bear Claw Road with me for a couple of days. When it was time for Bear Claw to leave, we embraced each other and renewed our friendship.

Scott said, "thank you for everything my friend."

Bear Claw said," thank you for my life my friend."

I rode off as Bear Claw watch. Before I went over the horizon I stopped and waved, He waved back, and both went their separate ways.

I cherish my time with the Black Foot, and I took my knowledge of what I learn from them back with me. It has been three days since Bear Claw and I departed the company, but that will not be the last time I will see him. I will need his help again later.

CHAPTER 5

The Journey Home

I was a few days from home, and excited to see my mother and father again. I have never been this long away from home before, and I have a lot to talk about.

The next day I broke camp mounted my horse and road off. One hour later I ran into a British patrol about five men. They ordered me to dismount and put my weapons on the ground. After I done what they said, they questioned me on what I am doing out here?

Scott said, "I am on my way to see my parents. I have been with some friends out west for a few years.

The Lieutenant said, "We are on the trail of a spy, and look where it led us to."

"And where is that" Scott side sarcastically.

The Lieutenant and the other four men move in to subdue me. I pull my knife and hatch out to defend myself. When they lower their musket on me, that is when I step forward to stab the first man that I came in reach of. I put my knife in his heart, the second man I hit across the neck with my hatchet. The Lieutenant drew his pistol to fire at me, but before he pulled the trigger, I grab the third man and move him between the pistol and me. The Lieutenant shot his own man in the back. I took the man's rifle that he was holding up, then I let him go. I spun around and with the butt of the rifle, I hit the fourth man in the head. Then I pointed the rifle at the Lieutenant and fired, killing him.

After the fight I realized what I had done. Thinking to myself, "WOW! The training that Bears Claw gave me paid off."

I suddenly realized that things back home must have gotten bad.

The spy that the British was looking for must have been on the wagon's I had dinner with, it is must have been one of the people. I smile at that though. So now it is a rush to see about my parents.

I wasted no time. I empty one of the dead man backpacks, fill it up with food and gun powder, I pick up one of the soldier's rifles, and pistol. Mounted my horse and continual East.

During the day I would ride, sometimes I would walk so I would not wear my horse out, and when I stop and make camp, I fix me something to eat, and in the morning prepare a snack before I break camp. I had to prepare myself and stay on the lookout in case I ran into more British soldiers.

Three days later I made camp still a few days from home, thanking my parents and how happy they will be to see me.

What else was going through my mind was the fear of war.

It was not long until trouble again caught up with me, it was the British again.

I made camp and sat down to eat. My gut was telling me that something was wrong. I remember that I had this feeling before when Bear Claw, me, and the hunting party came to the village when Koko, and Pita died. I remember Bear Claw saying.

"The spirits are letting you know something is wrong, I felt someone is looking for me."

It was the same feeling I had before we found the mountain man. This time I was not looking for someone, so someone must be looking for me. I kept my weapons on me when I unrolled my knapsack to bed down for the night.

The campfire was kept low, so I will not be seen at a distance, then fix my knapsack so it would appear I was sleeping in it. I slip into the darkness and wait.

An hour passed, and I was beginning to second guess myself. Then it happens. An arrow hit my knapsack then another and two more. I could not help to thank, if I ignored what I felt in my gut I would be dead.

I observe two Indians stepped out of the darkness, into my campfire light. I could tell what tribe they came from; they had two or three strips of paint on each side of their cheeks, their head was bald except for a strip of hair going from the top of their forehead to the back of the neck.

Following behind them was three soldiers, following the soldiers was a British office. It would appear I was being track. I overheard the officer say.

"This must be one of the people who attack our soldiers a few days ago."

I said to myself, "one of the people? Wouldn't he be surprised to find out that I was the only one?"

One of the Indian rolls my knapsack over and saw that I was not in it only stuffing. I immediately took my rifle aim and shot him while he was still kneeling over what he thought was me. I did not reload. Before the British officer could say anything to his men. The other Indian ran in the direction were the short came from. When the Indian got close enough, I shot him in the head with my pistol. As soon as I shot him, I dropped my pistol and moved around to my left, keeping it in the shadows.

The officer told his soldiers to fire pointing in the direction of where I killed the second Indian. The officer and all three soldiers open fire at his command. They started shouting in the dark. The officer gave the order to reload. That is when I attack.

I drew my knife and buried it in the chest of their officer, and quickly went to engage the three soldiers, they did not have time to reload.

But wait! I stop, the soldiers just stood there. I did not know what was going to happen next. The men just stood there; they did not move.

I found out later that without the officer they did not have any direction. The soldiers were confused. They did not know what the mission was, so they were lost.

I told them to pick a direction and leave I show them witch way was North. Then I said. "Go or die."

They started to go South then stopped, changed direction, and then went North.

After the men got out of sight I turn and continued to go East.

CHAPTER 6

Home Coming

Now understand, I was gone about three years, living with my friends the Black Foot tribe. My body has changed. I was bigger, strong, my hair was longer, and my clothes was different, on top of all that I had a British backpack.

When I walk into the town, I walk toward home, people did not realize who I was, and because of the backpack the towns people believe I was a British informer. Everyone was going out of their way to avoid me.

This town is usually friendly. People will walk up to you and help, by giving directions to what you are looking for. I ignore everyone, and mostly concentrate on getting home.

I started to have that strange feeling in my gut again. I become concerned. I went straight to my house. When I got home this feeling became almost unbearable.

First, I knocked and there was no answer, so I went in.

"Mom, Dad." Scott said.

Nothing, no responds.

"MOM, DAD." Scott yelled louder.

Still nothing I was not surprised that there was no one home, but I was surprised even more how dusty everything was. It would seem no one has been here for a long time. I know now that the house is empty. I went upstairs to see if I could find out why the house is like this. When I came down, there was four men waiting for me with their pistols pointed at my chest. I did not move because I needed answers.

No one said a word, the pistols were pointed at me in shock. You can see they are nervous. So, I better say something before that pistol goes off.

"Why are you men in my house?" Said Scott.

The man closest to me name is Jed Stone. He stood six feet tall, a little thin with short blond hair, and a thick mustache, his Son and I used to play in the mellow together when we were young. Jed did all the talking.

"Your House!?" said Jed.

I replied, "yes, my house."

Jed let me know, "this house belongs to the Martins, God rest their souls."

"What do you mean, God rest their soul!?" Said Scott very intents.

Still anger in his voice Jed said, "None of your business. Spy, traitor. You are to leave this house, or we will take you outside and shoot you. Just like you Red Coats did the Martins.

Rage field Scott's hart, this is a hell of a way to lean your mother and father was kill by the British. Scott forced himself to stay calm, and decided it was time for an introduction.

Scott turned to Jed and said, "Mr. Stone look at me, you know who I am, my name is Scott Edward Martin. Gertrude and Simon are my parents."

"Lier!" Scott Martin left and headed West." Said Jed aloud.

Scott step closer to Jed and said, "Look at me Mr. Stone I am Scott."

Jed stared at Scott hard then lowered his weapon and took another look at him.

"Scott is that really you?" It is good to see you, my boy. I am glad you are home. My goodness you have changed." Jed said as he held out his hand.

Both men shook hands.

"I am glad you are home?" Jed said again.

The other man who name is James said, "When I was a young boy, I used to steal apples from his father yard."

Then he got suspicious, "Why do you have a British backpack?" What Scott said next pleases them all.

"I had to kill a few of the red coats and took a backpack to carry my things, that I needed, but enough of me. What happen to my parents?" Ask Scott.

Jed let the other men know who Scott was, "Things are okay here, this is Scott Martin he used to live here, he is the Martins boy."

One of the men said, "I remember you, what a fine man you become."

"Thank you." said Scott.

The men knew what Jed is going to tell Scott. They all look at each other and walk out of the house. He turns back to Scott and said, "Let's sit down son."

Both men sat down in the living room, and nothing was said, until the last two men left.

Jed looked at Scott with pity in his eyes and said, "Your Mother and Father was shot, murdered in cold blood, in the town square as a public execution, to set the example to others. The Red Coats came through here two Months ago looking for recruit's, people who are loyal to their king. Your house was the first they came to. Your father must have seen them coming because he is the one who answers the door. The British officer was standing with his men, their rifle at their side."

The officer said, "In the name of our beloved King Gorge the third, you are to serve his troops and care for their needs."

The officer was expecting your father to react in a favorable manner instead his answer was.

"This is what I thank of your beloved King Gorge." Said Simon.

What Jed told Scott put concern in Scott face.

Jed said, "Than Simon spit on the ground, after, he attempts to close the door. The officer burst the door in and told Simon that you would pay for that insult. The officer grabs your father and pushes him into the street. Gertrude said a few words to the officer. What she said is unclear. Whatever it was he did not like it; he grabs her by the hair and threw her at the feet of Simon."

He told her, "You can join your husband."

The town was outraged. Your parents were made to stand with their backs against our well. Two men try to attack the soldiers, one was shot, the other beaten down and then was made to stand with your parent's. It was announced that they were arrested as spies and plotting against the king. The penalty is death.

When your father herd this, he plead with the officer to let your mother go, But the officer did not listen. He orders the soldiers to form a firing squad. Your mother and father along with everyone else drop to their knees to pray. The British used them as an example.

After they had been shot, the officer said. "We will be back here in three months. If this town does not comply with the British Empire, we will burn it to the ground, and that was two months ago."

A week later General George Washington came through here looking for men to join him to fight the Redcoats. Our young men were still angary about the executions, it was not hard to convince them to join up with General Washington.

Most of the young men went with him. At first, we were proud of them, but we soon realized our town is now unprotected.

Scott asks, "where are my parents buried?"

"We buried them on your property 200 yards from your back door." Said Jed.

I went to my parents' grave to say my goodbye. I spent a long-time mourning and telling them how much I love them, and how sorry I am that I was not here. I told them that their death will have repercussion.

When I left the grave site there was a plan forming in my mind. When I produced an idea. I went looking for Jed and found him in town coming out of one of the stores carrying a large feed bag.

Jed saw me coming and stopped what he was doing. He looked at me strange, he said, "it looks like you have something on your mind."

"Get together as many men as you can and meet me at my house." Said Scott.

CHAPTER 7

The Strategy

Jed came back with fifteen men most of them was in their forties and fifty's years of age. Some as young as fifteen. The men were very curious on what I had to say. I told them we are going to meet and fight the Red Coats before they get here. Everyone started to talk at once, they all wanted to know how we were going to fight an army that has never known defeat?

"And how are we going to do that?" Ask Jed.

I look at Jed with anger in my eyes and I answer.

"We are not going to wait until next month. We are going to take the fight to them. I made a promise to my parents that I will never forget them, and nothing will happen to our town."

"This is all the men that is left in the town." Said Jed.

Scott replied, "This is all the men we need. Come let me show you how to kill a Red Coat."

I knew I did not have much time to train them and meet the red coats before they came back.

A week later the fifteen men was as ready as they are going to be.

The town was nerves to see the rest of the men leave. However, I assure everyone that I have a backup plan. I told Jed to tell everyone in town they must get ready to leave. The people left behind; their job was to see that everyone was ready to leave when we got back.

Jed knew the direction from which the Red Coats came, and that is the way we went.

Our goal was to stop the British or slow them down long enough to give the towns people time to get away.

We been walking for three days before our Scouts came across the British army.

I also was acting as scout, and when we spotted the British it was the cavalry. They have already made camp for the night.

After I had seen how their camp was made. I went back to my men and from a plan. I told them how their camp was set up. Starting from the outside of the camp. The guards are posted around the camp and every fifty yards they walk back and forth along their post on the outside of the camp talking among themselves. The tents of the soldiers are set- up, so they surround the officer's tents. The horses are off to the right of the camp.

This is how we will proceed. Frist we will wait until the changing of the guards. Then we will move in and kill all the new guards. It will be four hours before the next change, this will give enough time to do a lot of damage. We do not want to alert them just yet. Jed you and four others will attend to their horses. They only have one guard there, kill the guard with your knife and release the horses, after the horse are gone, we will blow their gun power up. The confusion is when the rest of us will open fire on them. We will not reload, instead we will mount their horses and take off four miles down the road. There, we will set up an ambush for their Indian Scouts. The Scouts will be the first to arrive. All of them must die, none must escape.

My plan went off perfectly.

The one thing I did not count on was the number of officers the cavalry had. I do not know why so many officers were with them.

Before they reach our town all the officers must be killed. Or they will burn down the town, that is why all must die. But we will concentrate on the Indian first.

I decided that every time we engage the enemy, we will have to make sure an officer is killed. Starting tonight.

Later that night we move in; with my bow the guards are killed by my arrows. Jed took care of the soldier guarding the horses and took them away to be used by us.

We waited until one of the officers came out of the tent and we opened fire. The officer fell dead. But the shot awakens everyone. When the soldier stood up the rest of my men fire on them. After we shot the soldiers, we retreated to our rendezvous. One of the soldiers discovered that the horses are gone and reported it to the officers, that the horse our missing, and the attackers fled, the officer in charge know it will be useless to follow whoever did this we cannot track them in the dark instead he said, "Double the guards, we will move out in the morning."

After we ran to where Jed was waiting with the horse and road off.

The next morning, we set our ambush up and waited. We did not have to wait long. The Indian scouts was well ahead of the Red Coats. The only thing that did not change is the distance between the Mohegan, and the Red Coats. The distance is the same as it was when they had their horses. If the Mohegan were to attack, the cavalry could respond quickly on horseback. But now that the cavalry is on foot with the same distance, the cavalry could not react as fast, a mistake that they will regret.

When the Mohegan stepped into our ambush. I made the first shot with my bow. The arrow land in the chest of one Indian, the second one I engage him with my knife, the other two shot by Jed and the rest of his men. When the British found their scouts lying in the road dead. The captain said to one of the officers, "we will never find the town you mentioned to me. One of the Lieutenant steps forward and said, "I know the way to the town of these rebels,"

Scott and his man-made camp, after they went over what happen today. Less recap. The British are without their horses and their Indian scouts. Plus, one of the officers is dead.

Now we turn our attention to killing the rest of the officer.

We kept an eye on the Red Coats during the day. When they made camp. We waited until it was late, and they all turned in for the night.

As we approach the British camp, we notice the guards were nervous, because of what happened the night before, and to their scouts.

After the change of the guard, we act.

We move in killing all the guards quietly, I notice two officers talking outside of their tent. One went inside, while the other stayed outside smoking his pipe.

That was my chance, I put an arrow in the neck of the waiting officer. When his friend came out of his tent, he saw his friend lying dead, before he had a chance to react, I put an arrow in his chest, and another one in the same place before he hit the ground.

We were going to blow up their food supply, then I was surprised to see another wagon with gunpowder. So, we took as much food as we could carry. Move the supply wagon close to the wagon with the gunpowder. I opened one keg to pour power over the rest of the kegs and made a trial of gunpowder away from the wagons into the woods. We had to move quickly because it was a matter of time before the two officers would be discovered.

Fifteen of my men was assign to a tent where the troops sleep. I told them to shoot the first man that comes out.

Everyone was ready, I lit the fuse, and it happened, BOOM! BOOM! BOOM!

It was louder than I expected, the wagon blew up and everyone in the camp felt it. The soldiers came out of their tents to see what had happen, and was short immediately, most of them died, the others were wounded but died later.

My men and I did not reload, we had to get to our new rendezvous point as fast as they can. All arrived safely, "everyone is present and accounted for." Said Jed. Then we left as fast as we could.

The British was confused, all their scouts where dead, and some of their officers including their Commanding officer. The new officers in charge demanded to know who, and where the attack was coming from. When the officer did not get any answers, he called for the sergeant of the guard.

The sergeant of the guard reported, "Sergeant McFee reporting sir." The sergeant is a war veteran and knows his stuff.

The captain wanted to know what happened.

The sergeant said, "All the guards are dead sir, some of the men died as they were coming out of their tents."

"All of the guards?" Ask the Captain.

"Yes, sir all of them." Said sergeant McFee.

The Captain Order, "Send a patrol out to find out where this attack is coming from. Then form a buried detail and buried the dead, And Sergeant."

"Yes sir." Said the Sergeant McFee.

"Tell the guards to kill anything that moves." Said the Captain.

While the British was getting organize.

My men and I sat forward in making our next move.

Scott said, "Okay, everyone gathers round and listens up. They are going to send out patrols, we cannot slip into their camp anymore because they will be ready for us, and we cannot stand against the British in an open battle, so we must pick where, and how we will engage them. So, here is what we are going to do.

We are going to kill their patrols; we will have a better change in beating them with less men, the more patrols we kill, the fewer men they will have. So, we will take our position behind the trees and rocks, we will keep out of sight until they are well in our sights. This time we wait until they come to us."

It was not long before the patrol came onto our ambush.

Now the key to a good ambush is patience, you will have to wait until your enemy gets in the right spot so no one can escape.

When the British was in the right position. I gave the commanded, "FIRE!"

It happens so fast the British did not have time to return fire.

We kill all but two men, one of the two men is wounded in the arm, and the other was frozen scared.

We took their weapons and sent them on their way back to what was left of their camp with a message.

The officer retrieve the message and it read, for murdering the good people of our town, we sentence all of you to death. This was to put fear in them, and it worked.

After our encounter with the patrol, we made camp away from the ambush.

My men were happy and satisfied, and that is a problem.

I had to address the men and bring them back to reality.

"We kill a lot of redcoats tonight, and we have a lot more to do, do not thank that because we kill a few redcoats that is it, and do not forget the reason we are out here. They kill our friends, and my family. They must pay for that!" Said Scott very angrily.

Scott closed his eyes and took a deep breath to calm himself down. Then Scott said calmly, "Let us recap, we took away their gun power, their horses, killed all their Scouts, and couple of their officers. Today we are going to kill more"

One of the men spoke out.

"I have an idea; I saw a hornet nest in the woods we can put a bag over it and throw it into their formation.

Scott added, "very good, and while the redcoats mind is on the bees, we will take that opportunity to kill a few more officers"

Scott asks the man, "take someone with you to get the nest. The man chose his good friend he knew for years. The two men, one with the idea about the hornet nest, and another man, his friand went into the woods to retrieve the nest.

The other man asks, "how are you going to get the hornets to behave when you take their home?"

"Easy, give me your canteen, and tear off a piece of your shirt and wrap it around a stick." Said the man with the idea.

The other man follows the direction he rips his shirt and raps the cloth around a stick, took the canteen and pour water carefully on the cloth but not to soak it, then he made a small fire and lit it. The touch did not flame, it smolders, and gave off a lot of smoke. He gave the touch to his friend and spoke.

"Hold it up to the nest, the smoke will keep them calm." Said the man with the Idea.

His friend said, "How do you know how to do this?"

"We had a cookout one day. The fire we built to cook our food was under a nest of hornets we did not know until it was time to leave. We were not stung because of the smoke from the fire." Said the man with the idea.

His friend said sarcastically, "Okay that's comforting, you know if things go wrong, you will be left up there, and I will be down the road."

Both men laughed. The friend held the torch toward the nest. The smoke rose very thick. The hornets started to buzz. The man with the idea climbed the tree. The buzz was becoming louder but none of the hornets came out. He put a burlap sack over the nest and tied it. Then he broke the limb that the nest was attached to and climbed down with the hornet nest in tool.

The next morning Scott told his men, "This ends today."

That was the first thing that came out of his mouth."

Jed step forward and said, "Scott, there is something I need to tell you. One of the officers is the very one who order the execution in the town square."

This renews Scott anger. Scott asks his men, "Do anyone know what this officer looks like?"

Most of the fifteen men said, "I do."

"New plan." Scott said immediately.

The officer that killed our friends, my parents, must live to stand trial, then he is be hung by his neck. One of you will have to go back to our town to see how everyone is doing with the packing. Jed it must be you, the town people listen to you. Get them ready Jed, because after the British find out what we have done. They will send the entire regiment to our town and believed me they will kill everyone and burn the town down."

Jed just nods his head in agreement. Then mounted one of the horses and road off toward the direction of the town.

One of the men ask, "what are we going to do now?"

Scott answer was, "we will make our stand a mile down the road near the lake. There is a branch that hands over the road put the nest on that branch with a rope on it that lead into the woods when the redcoats are directly under it, I will give the single, you will pull the rope and the nest will fall to the ground releasing the hornets. Once the hornets attack the redcoats, we will open fire from our hiding place. This time we will reload and fire again. After we fire the second time reload but hold your fire. I will ask for their surrender."

Scott raised his voice and said, "Okay all of you have your orders let's move out and find our position for the ambush."

After Scott and his man arrive at the site of the ambush everyone found a place, the trap was set, A man came to Scott and said, "All the men are at their post sir."

"Very good, now the hard part, we wait." We did not have to wait long.

Just before dawn in the British camp the Sargent of the guard came to the now officer in charge and ask.

"Should I wake up the man sir?"

"No, let them sleep a little longer, they had a rough night the men need their rest," side the officer.

This is no ordinary officer. This is the same officer that had Scott Martin's parents killed. He is now a senior officer.

In the camp the officers talk among themselves, "We are the only two officers left. Here is our option, we are out of food, no horse, and running low on gun power." Said the junior officer.

"There is a town about a day from here, we will get supplies there, or we can turn back and try to make it back to the fort. It would be better to push on to the town. I feel all that is happen to us, we will fine our answers there." Said the senior officer.

The junior officer said, "The rebels are just ahead of us waiting for us to make them pay for what they have done. If we start our march and keep moving all day, I believe that we can surprise them."

The officer in charge yell, "Sargent."

The Sergeant was a seasoned war veteran and no strangers to the ways of war. He has been in a lot of campaigns, and served a lot of good officers, good officers except this one. The senior lieutenant was arrogant and only cared about himself and what Glory he could achieve, and in this case this lieutenant cannot think of anything but burning down the town he visited before.

The senior lieutenant said to the sergeant, "get the man ready for a hard march all day. We should reach the town by sunset. Our attackers, those so-called rebels are not your ordinary rebels. This is the doing of an organized group. These men came from the very town for which we are headed."

The junior officer was wondering, he asks, "Why do you believe that?"

"I dealt with them before just months ago. They were very disloyal, and disrespectful to King George III. I was forced to make an example of the townspeople. But what I do not understand how they got so organize so quickly." Said the senior officer.

While the two officers were talking, little did they know. I had a spy watching everything the officer said and did. My spy overheard all their plans. After that he found his way back to his horse, mount and headed back to our camp.

Later the British started their march, by noon they were tired and in much needed rest. It was too late; they walked into our trap.

The branches with the huge hornet nest were hanging over the middle of the formation. I gave the single, and down came the nest. When it hit the ground, the sack burst open and immediately a cloud of hornets rose from the bag. At first everyone around was in shock, that is when the hornets went to work, everyone started to run in all directions, no one found comfort. I gave the signal to fire we opened with a furious round. A lot of the redcoats died or wounded. They could not return fire because of the hornets. The redcoats ran and jumped into the nearby lake. The British was trying to stay underwater until the hornets leave, only coming up when they had to get some air.

During this time, we move the nest a few yards away from the road, then we pick up the rest of their gunpowder after we all mounted our horses and road hard until we reach our town.

When we arrived, everyone was still getting things together. I told my men to spread the word. Pack just food, water, tools, and clothes. I do not want anything left that the redcoats can used. We move out as soon as we can. We are heading West.

To my surprise the color people of our town were just standing and looking at everyone packing.

Scott said, "this means you too. You are still apart of this town."

Two of the town's men step forward, they notice that they were not moving. I just watched to see how this was going to play out.

The first man said with a strong voice, "What are you people waiting for a special invitation, you men and women has always been part of this town our children played together, your children even went off to fight against the British. What makes you think everything stops now? I will send some men and wagons to help you pack."

Scott thanking to himself, "it's a great thing to be excepted." All the Black man smiles and turn to get ready.

The second man said, "I'll go with them to see how many wagons we need."

As he walked away, he said aloud. "No one get left behind." That is a catchy saying, it might just catch on."

I was proud of my town, it was a wonderful place to live, and the people are like no other.

We left behind nothing. By the time the British soldiers arrives in town. They were exhausted, hungry, and miserable.

They took precautions and stopped at the edge of town. The officers sent in their sergeant and a squad of soldiers to make sure there were no traps, and to secure any surplus. The sergeant sent a man back with a report.

The massager said, "The town is empty sir."

"What do you mean empty? This was a huge town, a few months ago. What happen?" Replied the Officer.

"We can thank about that later let's see what supplies we can fine." The other officer said.

The junior officer said to his senior, "Tell me something, what did you do to these people to make them so angry?"

"I don't know what you are talking about." The senior officer said as he steps forward to say something to the messenger.

"Tell the sergeant to see if he can fine any supply's we will join him soon." Said the senior officer.

At the same time, the junior officer stepped aside to drink his water. While doing this he overheard two soldiers talking.

"This is the same town that the Lieutenant executed the old couple to set the example for the rest of the town."

After that, the Lieutenant immediately went to the senior Lieutenant and said, "I just heard the men talking that you killed an old couple in this town, and I bet the rebels are from here. The couple you killed is why the rebels are out for revenge. All of this could have been prevented if it were not for your ego."

The senior officer snap back and said, "No your place Lieutenant, they disrespect our king, and the penalty for that is death."

The junior officer raises his voice, "Was it worth all this!? Because of your misuse of your authority, and the misrepresentation of England and our King George. I am relieving you of duty and your command. and placing you under arrest. If I knew of this at first, we could have prevented the death of our comrades."

"Sargent," yelled the junior officer.

Hearing what took place between the two officers, the Sargent answer immensely, "yes sir." In a loud voice.

The junior officer pointed at the senior officer and said to the Sargent, "place this officer under arrest."

The Sargent replied, this time his voice was not as loud but surprisingly pleasant, "yes sir."

"The charge is misrepresenting England, and unbecoming an officer," said the junior Lieutenant."

The Sargent called two of his soldiers over and said, "relived the Frist Lieutenant of his weapon and stay with him." The soldiers flank the senior Lieutenant on each side.

The junior Lieutenant, who is now in charge, said, "let me see if I can stop the killing."

The Lieutenant walks into town along with his hands over his head. "Let's see if I can fix this." The Lieutenant saying to no one in particular." He saw Scott coming down the street with a white flag.

The Lieutenant said aloud, "finally someone to talk to, I except your surrender?"

Scott smiled and said, "that is funny, and I came to you, to accept yours. You have an officer with you, a Lieutenant I believe. Turn him over to us, and we will give you and your men food and enough ammo to get home. If not you and your man will die, and we will still have him."

The junior Lieutenant said, "the officer in question is under a rest for crimes against the crown. He will stand trial when we get back to our command."

Scott looks at the man extremely hard and said, "Yes, he will stand trial, but the crime he committed is murder. Turn him over to us, and we will look after your wounded, the choice is yours."

"I am sorry sir we don't just hand over our officers." Said the Lieutenant.

Without backing down, Scott insists, "understand this sir, we will take him! If you do not hand him over more of your men will die. So, either way we will have him. Thank about its sir. Look at your men they cannot stand another battle. You will lose, and we will have him anyway. You can save lives today." Said Scott.

The Lieutenant though about continued the fight but, the wellbeing of his men dictated otherwise, his men are hungry and in need of a doctor. He pauses, while looking at Scott then he says reluctantly.

"I yield to you sir. Will you allow me to make him ready?"

Scott answer, "Yes sir go right ahead I trust you will not do anything unwise?"

"You have my word as an officer of the crown." Said the Lieutenant."

The lieutenant could not produce any other way out of this without any moor of his man being killed. He went back to his men and said, "lower your weapons."

The Lieutenant that was a prisoner said aloud to the men in hope to gain support, "this officer is surrendering you to the rabbles. Fight, do not become a prisoner."

"The only person that is surrendering is you, the person that cause the death of our comrades. The regret I have is, I cannot bring you up on charges myself." Said the junior Lieutenant.

After saying that, the Officer in charge told his men, "Turn over the prisoner to the rebels."

Two of the British soldiers escort the prisoner into town and handed him over to the towns people. The prisoner stood trial and was found guilty. He was hung by the neck until he was dead. After the trail Scott told the town's doctor, to look after the redcoat's wounds. I thought I would feel better, but I did not. I was still angry. War is coming, and I will do my part.

Three of Scott's men gathered all the redcoat's weapons and put them in a wagon, and they took off back down the road with the wagon, from which they came.

The next day Scott's men escort the soldiers out of town.

Scott told the Lieutenant, "You will find your weapons and some gun power a day and a half walk from the directions you came to town."

Now understand when all of this was going on, we wear still not at war so that is why we did not hold the redcoats. I sent word to the Colonial Army, to inform them what happened, and the direction they went.

We know that British soldiers will be back, and we also know how angry they will be when they see one of their officers hanging from a tree on the way into town.

We gather supplies and equipment from the town and prepare for the journey. The men made sure the British have nothing to use. All of us are about to take a journey to a place where the Black Foot had shown me.

I spent two days making sure there was nothing left, or any clue about their about. We were about to leave when we were surprised to see a colonial army come to our town led by General George Washington.

General Washington receives my report, and came looking for me, the General ask, "who is Mr. Scott Martin?"

General Washington was impressed when he read my report on how we defeated the redcoat with untrained man, and without loosening anyone. He wanted to meet me.

General Washington and I talk for quite a while, I learn that the General has a plan to train fighting men and push them to their limits and beyond. And to do this he needs instructors who know how to manage this. The General told me of great warriors that demand respect.

The warriors are called Samurai, the place is called Japan.

CHAPTER 8

Making of the Camp

I was surprised by what came next. The General ask, "Would you be interested in going to Japan on behalf of our government? Your mission is to ask their emperor to borrow their instructors to train our men for war."

I could not believe what I was hearing, I had to ask, "Why me and not a diplomat?"

"When you can persuade a few men, who were out man, and out gun to take on the British army, oh yeah, now that, is the man I need." Said the General.

General Washington did not stop there. "You can do your Country a great justice. I will give you the rank of colonel, you will go to Japan to represent me, and bring back some instructor, or learn what we need to get an advantage over the British in combat. Learn their ways in battle, how they train and bring that knowledge back here. It would help us with our cause. We are on the brink of war against a highly trained army. We need an edge, Son."

"I would do as you wish. But it would have to wait after I relocate my town." Said Scott.

"Very well my boy, take care of your people and after, do what your country needs of you."

After General Washington and I had our talk, he gave me my orders, and the rank of Colonel I am to report to a ship called the Portages on the West Coast, he gave me a map to where he is docked. The captain will already have his orders. He has been to Japan many times, so he will brief me on their customs.

I do not know what I was about to get myself into with the trip to Japan, but I will find out when the time comes.

When General Washington and I parted company. My orders must be put on hold; my priority is to get my town's people to safety. I was thinking to myself, "Should the town be touch?" I decided no.

I inform my men, "leave the town standing it will cause them to delay a little longer. It will take the redcoats time to figure out what happened.

The men that were with me made sure the town was empty. There was nothing the redcoats could use, but before we left to join the others, I wanted to clean myself up. I got a haircut bath and put on a change of cloth.

I was in my parents' house, in my old room. I could not help thinking how much danger the townspeople are in. The British will not let this pass they will be back and this time they will be more prepared; the towns people will not have a chance.

What can I say to everyone? Where can I take them? And how would I approach them? And would they listen to me? All these questions were going through my head. I do know one thing I have to get these people away from here, So, I sent for Jed.

When Jed came to Scott houses, Scott asks Jed to sit down in the living room, when they were comfortable Scott told Jed, "I wanted to speak to you privately, I have a mission for you. You are to ride west to find an Indian tribe called the black foot, ask to speak to Bear Claw, tell him who you are, and that I sent you. Tell him all that has happened. I will rendezvous with him in three days when we used to go fishing. I am sorry old friend, but I need you to go now."

After I cleaned myself up, I came out of my house, a lot of people were waiting for me. When I stepped out onto my porch everyone cheered.

Scott was surprised, "thank you, you honor me. However, I am deeply sorry to inform you that this is not over." Everyone got quiet.

I inform everyone, "The British will be back with a bigger force. This time they will be unstoppable. The redcoats will burn this town down, and kill everyone here, for what we have done to them, we are now on barrow time."

One of the men yelled out, "What can we do, this town is our life?"

Scott replied, "So we take the town with us, the town is not buildings, it is you, the people are the town. We can move town. Wherever we settle will be our town. I have already sent word ahead to some friend of mine to help us. We will go where we can be safe from the war. Where you can farm, trade, fish, and hunt. You can build a town the way you want.

Look, I know you do not want to leave but understand this. You have your wife, children, and Grandchildren to care for.

And we do have an advantage. It will be a long time before they find their way back to the Fort, then they will rest. After, they will plan an attack on this town with a larger regiment to do only one thing, which is to wipe this town out. We made the red coats look bad, and they do not like looking bad. That is why we must move this town!"

At first no one said a word. Then one of the men walk toward me stop turn and look at everyone. When he had the crowd's attention, he said in a loud voice turning back to me saying.

"Will you lead us?"

That made me happy to hear what he said.

Scott replied, "I will. I will stay with you until we get to the place, I pick for us; we will make our home there. After, I will go on the mission that General Washington gave me. If we leave now the Redcoats will not be able to tell which way, we went."

All our wagons lined up, one behind the other. There is one more thing I need to do. I grab a large blanket and tie it to the last wagon in a way that half of it touches the ground, so it can drag. This will erase the tracks of the wagon wheels and horse.

The wagon train was long and slow, but we had time on our side. The towns people left way before the British return. We never heard from them again. I assume the blanket worked; our tracks were covered well.

We headed northwest. The whole trip was rough at first. This is something that is new, people are not used to traveling in this manner.

Everyone has stop talking about the British, and what we done. The talk is now about where we are going, what to expect, and when we will get there.

After a few days, the people start to get irritable and have doubts. Some of the men started to question me. They believed that I did not know what I was doing. Things started to get ugly, until we saw my friends Black Foot. At first, I thought it was a scouting party, it was not until I talked to them when I found out it was a hunting party.

They have been watching us from a far for quite some time. The towns people did not see the party until they wanted to be seen.

When the hunting party decided to approach us, the towns people got very nerves. They did not know what to expect. They only headed things about the Indians, and now they see them in real life. The men grab their guns.

I stood in front of them and said, "you ask me to lead you. This is part of my plan; these men are my friends. Just stay calm and everything will be all right."

As the hunting party got closer everyone was surprised to see Jed riding with them.

Scott went on to say, "We need these people to help us, because where we are going to settle is on their land."

Hearing what Scott said all the men lower their weapons.

"I'll go out to talk to them." Said Scott.

Scott road out to meet the Indians, hoping it is his friends.

The Indians was led by Bear Claw, with Jed beside him. Scott was pleased to see his friend. The first thing that came out of Bear Claw mouth was.

"Did we come at a bad time." Said Bear Claw with a big smile on his face.

We both started to laugh aloud, this eases the tension of the towns people. Bear Claw and his party were invited to our camp for dinner.

When we approach the wagons, the men came out to meet us without their weapons.

We all made camp together, I put all the small talk aside and got to the point. I informed Bear Claw what had happened, and that I was on my way to ask his father permission to saddle on his land to the north. I wish to make a city there, to keep my people safe from the war back East.

Bear Claw agree to ride with me back to talk to his father only if I, and few of the men join them in a hunt.

Scott said, "It is very important to get answers right away because the British maybe tracking us."

"You and I will go together." Said Bear Claw.

Bear Claw look around the wagons and said, "tell me, where are your young brave?"

"They left to fight in the war, after what had happened." Said Scott. Bear Claw side to his Braves, "Continual the hunt and some of Scott's people will join you. Then take them to our village."

I told the townspeople what the plan was, I will make arrangements on the land we are about to occupy. You will join me soon after the hunt. We will need the meat for the upcoming months, do not worry you will be safe."

Jed and a few of the men volunteered to go on the hunt. One of the men ask, "what are we hunting?"

What I told him was, "a wonder, you have never seen before." I left it at that with a smile.

Bear Claw and I left right away, as we rode off, one of the towns men and one brave went a head of the hunting party to Scout.

Now understand, the two men could not speak to each other because of the language, so they used hand sign.

The two roads were about an hour together saying nothing until the brave gave a signal to stop.

Jed using sign ask, "Why are we stopping?"

The brave did not say a word he just dismounts, secured his horse, and beckoned the man to follow. Jed dismounted, and after securing his horse ran to the brave side, here the brave was waiting for him at the bottom of a small hill. At first the two men walk halfway up the hill. Near the top the brave got on his stomach and started to crawl the Jed did the same and crawl the rest of the way up.

When the two men got to the top, they look down into the valley and their eyes widen in disbelieve. The towns man side in a whisper.

"Oh my God." He said in amazement.

They were looking at miles and miles of Buffalo.

The Brave smiled at Jed in approval. He touches Jed on the shoulder to get him out of his trance, then the brave gesture him to come back down the hill. They both ran back to the horses, mounted them, and joined the rest of the hunting party.

The two men reported to the rest of the party what, and where, they seen Buffalo.

But Jed was still excited about what he saw; he could not put words together.

A towns man said, "settle down man, and tell us what you saw."

Jed realizes how excited he was, and he took a deep breath and made himself calm down.

"What I am excited about is Buffalo. Real Buffalo, we always have heard stories about Buffalo from people coming from the West but never seen them. They are magnificent!" Said Jed.

"Buffalo! What is a Buffalo?" Ask another man.

"A Buffalo is like a different looking cow, with short horns and a hump in its back but bigger. It is what we came to hunt." Said Jed.

"Are their enough to go around?" ask another man.

Jed looks at the man and said excitedly, "I believe we will have plenty!" We will let the braves go in first, then we will follow." Said Jed.

The hunting party was ready, as planned the Black foot attack first. The town people watch as the Black Foot engage the Buffalo after seeing what they were doing and how. Then they join the hunt.

After a successful hunt, the hunting party made their way back to their camp.

The whole hunting party was excited about how the day went. When the men inform the rest of the towns people how the hunt went. It was told to everyone that we have enough meat and skin to last through the winter.

Later that evening the brave went on ahead of us to prepare for our arrival.

The experience was great with the Buffalo. We will not be Hungary for a long time.

We slowly made our way to the Black Foot village with Jed leading us.

While all of this was going on, I will tell you what happened with Bear Claw, and when we left the camp to see Bear Claw's father.

There was no time to waste, Scott knowing that the British will be trying to track them.

Riding hard, Scott and Bear Claw reach his father's camp.

After telling Bear Claw's Father Chief Mingan what happened, I asked for help.

Chief Mingan was still grateful to Scott for saving his son's life. He put his hand on Scott's shoulder and said one word, "family." That is how Chief Mingan looks at me, as family. He sat down and talked to his consul for a while on the advice of Bear Claw.

"Take Scott and his people to the north where we go for the summer.

There they can build a life for his people." Said Chief Mingan.

"I wish I could stay longer but I have to get back to my people." Said Scott.

"I told my braves to bring your people here after the hunt." Said Bear Claw.

When the towns people showed up, we stayed for one night to honor Chief Mingan. The next morning, we left early.

The Black Foot Tribe went south and. Bear Claw escort us North.

The trip to the north went well. The land that the Chief recommended to us was massive enough to build a large city, we name our new town, The Camp.

Soon after, we arrived at our destination. I had to take a step back and see how beautiful the land was. What the Chief gave us was prime land, we have enough man to build a Large city and plus it was not long after before we discovered gold.

But that is another story.

Scott has everyone's attention around the campfire. But before Scott could speak again Yalonda interrupted.

"That is an amazing story about how the Camp got started but tell us Scott. How did The Five come about? "Ask Yalonda.

Well, after we got to the Camp underway, I left, went, and made legal claim for the land.

Yalonda interrupted again.

"If the Black Foot gave all this land to you, why do you feel that you have to have a claim?" Said Yalonda.

Scott answered, "Well that is a good question. The white man looks at all this land as open territory, and the land is up for grabs, so if I file a claim. I will be cover in both worlds."

Yalonda nodded to let Scott know she understood.

Scott went on with his story.

As you know General Washington ask me to go to Japan to recruit warriors and bring someone back to train his man how to fight. Well, I decided to take that challenge.

Bear Claw and some braves were with us since we first arrived at this new land, they showed us where to fish, and hunt, and what game is in the area, also how to trap it.

When it was time to leave, a horse was given to me, strong and has a lot of spirit. A black stallion that seems to stand out among all the rest, it was a gift from Bear Claw.

I mount my stallion who I named Rock. Bear Claw also mounts his horse whose name is Windbreaker. His horse is an appaloosa. An appaloosa is the color of a horse that has black and white spots.

Bear Claw said, "I will stay with you until you board your ship, you have not been that far west before, so I will be your guide."

We said our goodbyes to the townspeople and left. The trip west was pleasant and exciting.

CHAPTER 9

The Journey West

I see things that I have never seen before. We avoided unfriendly Indians that may cause trouble, and we travel light, so we can make good time. We ate off the land, rabbits, and other small games.

Bear Claw was true to his word, he stayed with me until I reached the West Coast. We found the ship that General Washington told us about and went aboard.

Once we reached our destination, I was a little nervous. The ship was large, it had two main sales and one hundred cannons, it took a lot of people to run this ship, how many? I never knew or cared. This ship is made for war. The name of the ship was The Monika. I found out later that this ship had once belong to the British. When the British had it, it was named The Queen Charlotte. Capt. Jeff never let on how he came across the ship, and I never pressed the subject. Bear Claw and I went aboard it under her new name. The first mate is the first to approaches us, he is a tall man, slim, and with a scar on the side of his check. I never ask him how he got it, and he never talks about it. I told him who I was. "My name is Scott Martin; I am here under orders of General George Washington to see Capt. Jeffery Moor."

The first mate replied, "We were expecting you, but we were not told it was two of you."

My Friend will not be staying, he is here to see me on my way."

The First mate introduce himself, "my name is Steve Mitchell. I am the first mate of The Monika, a find ship. The captains order me to give you a tour when you come aboard. It looks like you made suitable time, we were expecting you in a couple of days."

"I had a good guide." Scott motion to Bear Claw.

After the tour of the ship was over, I said my goodbyes to Bear Claw, and I went to meet the captain.

We went to the Captains Quarters. Stave knocks on the door. A voice on the other side said. "Come in."

Stave open the door and step aside. I walked in and he closed the door behind us.

The first mat introduces me to Captain Jeffery More, "Meet Clonal Scott Martin. Sir, this is the man we have been waiting for."

The captain was not at all what I expected, in fact just the opposite. The captain is an impeccably dress man clean shave and well educated. I can tell he was an educated man his quarters are well kept. It is like stepping into a library. He has books from various parts of the world.

On a table to the left of his Desk, there are charts, maps, and more books.

Captain Jeffery Moore extended his hand and said, "Welcome aboard."

We shook hands after, he turned to his first mate and said, "Now that Col. Scott is here, make ready to get under way, we should not waste time." The First Mate replied, "aye sir."

Then he turned and walked out. Captain Moore turned to me and said, "Please have a seat," he pointed to a comfortable chair across from his desk.

As I sat down, he began to speak about the mission.

But first he said, "general Washington must think very highly of you to send you on such a mission. Do you have any idea where you are going or the people you are about to encounter?"

Scott shook his head no and said, "Only thing he told me. There was a land of great warriors and to bring back some to help train our men for the upcoming war."

Captain Moore laughed aloud and said, "General Washington has no clue what he is sending you into. But you are in luck." Said Captain Moore.

Scott frown and said, "and how am I in luck?"

Captain Moore said, "because I know the customs and speak the language."

Scott smile and said, "how fortunate."

"Did you think I was just pick out of a hat?" Said Captain Moore. Both men then laughed aloud.

Captain Moore went on to say. "But look at you. General Washington wrote me about what you did against the British, he is impress. From what he said, you might be just the person that will convince these people to cooperate and believe me that is a feat I will have to see. Although I really do not believe this can happen"

Scott said, "Why did you say that you don't thank this can happen?"

"No. I do not believe you can, but from what General Washington has written about you. I am willing to take my ship across the largest ocean in the world to see you try. Said Captain Moore.

Scott said, "Well thank you for your vote of confidence, but I can handle myself very well."

Yes, I can see that, but you are still going to need me. And doing this journey I am going to teach you on the custom and language, and just maybe that will be enough to give you an edge, and not get us kill." Said Captain Moore.

CHAPTER 10

Japan

The two men talk a little more. After, Captain Moore called for one of his crew men to show Scott to his quarters.

Before I left Captain Moore Quarters he Said, "Get settle in Colonel. Although the trip is long, you have a lot to learn. I just hope we have enough time."

"Don't worry Captain I am a quick learner." Replied Scott.

Then Scott smiled and walked out.

Doing the time that I was unpacking, I got a strange feeling in my gut. I could not tell if it was good or bad. I would know when I get to this place called Japan.

Our journey across the Pacific Ocean was really breath taking. The water was calm, the weather was pleasant, and our sails were full.

Halfway to our destitution we drop anchored at a group of Islands. Captain Jeff turned to Scott and said, "you are going to like this. We are here for supplies; we will not be staying long. So, while we have here allowed me to show you what haven might be like, we are going to take a quick look at paradise. This place is fantastic.

We stayed a day on the island, and while we were there, Captain Moore showed me things that were unbelievable. I can only describe what I saw in one word. Beautiful.

The native as a hold are very friendly and peaceful, however, the women, are lovely.

Captain Moore said, "it's like this all year round."

We picked up what supplies we needed and continued our journey.

"You could have skipped the part about how beautiful the woman is" said Sylvia playfully.

Everyone around the campfire laughs loudly.

"Sorry, my love." Scott said smiling.

It was hard to leave such a place out of my story, but once we got our supplies, we had to Continue our mission. While we were on that island, I seen creatures I had never seen before, and Captain Moore was familiar with all of them. We left a place I would want to see again.

During the trip Captain Moore have been teaching me on how to act in the country of Japan.

It seems the native of Japan are very polite, but do not insult the Samurai in any way.

"What is a Samurai." Ask Scott.

The Samurai are the ones we are trying to recruit. They are quite easy to insult; so, please listen to everything I say. You must bow to everyone before you speak to them and bow after.

The Japanese valve respect, bravery, and honor.

"The people of this country sound interesting, I want to learn as much about this country that I can before we get there." Said Scott.

Captain Moore also told me about the rank structure.

Captain Moore said, "Now listen carefully. There is Knewmeaning, housemen, they were the administrators or vassal. The Mounted Samurai, only high-ranking samurai warriors could fight on horseback. The foot soldiers are self-explanatory. Now the rank of Shogun is the highest rank of the Samurai. He answers only to the emperor."

Scott said, "Since General Washington is the highest rank in my country, and I have his ear, then I will present myself as a General. The same as Shogun. I will talk about my mission to know lesser rank."

"That might work, or we might get killed, it is hard to tell with these Samurai." Said Captain Moore.

As we approach Japan, a ship met us just offshore, the ship is full of Samurai. It was a heavy and awkward vessel not very seaworthy. It was something you use close to shore. The ship stops us, and The Captain ask. "What business do you have here?"

Captain Jeff bowed, and in their language responded. "I have important official business for your honorable and most high emperor." The Samurai Captain asks, "is the emperor expecting you?"

Captain Moore bowed again and said, "No, we were sent by our Emperor."

The Samurai Captain answered in a stern voice. "Then you are not allowed here."

Captain Moore bowing a third time and said, "I respect your decision turning the emperor friend away, if you would please tell the emperor that his friend Captain Jeffery Moor give his respects, and you did your job by sending us away without an invitation. It is good that the emperor has someone to speak to him.

The Samurai Captain recognizes this man, Jeffery Moore. He is not only the emperor's friend; he is the emperor's close friend. He has the privilege to come and go as he pleases.

He pauses for a long time staring at Captain Moore.

Captain Moore returns the stare without blinking; he knew the first one to speak loses his advantage with this conversation.

The Samurai turned to talk to someone behind him and pointed to Captain Moore, he became very pale, and was trying to hide how nervons he was.

He instructed Captain Moore, "You may dock your ship, but you are not to leave it until I return.

Captain Moore bowing again and said, "Thank you, you are wise.

The samurai ship docks first, then Captain Moore ship docks alongside of it. When you see the ships side by side you can see that everyone was amazed how large Captain Moore ship in compared to theirs. Captain Moore heard bits and pieces of what they were saying. They were looking and pointing at the distinct parts of the ship until the captain of the samurai ship told his men to attend to their work. Both captains look at each other, and both men bow. Then Captain Moore turned to Scott and said, "You just might get to see the emperor after all."

Captain Moore told Scott everything that he said, "I challenge his authority. When he reported that he sent me away without informing the Emperor I was here. The emperor will have his head."

Scott asks, "why."

"I saved the emperor's life a while back. I will not go into details because I was told to keep it a secret. Only me, the emperor, and two of the Generals know. After I saved his life the Emperor and I became the best of friends, and I have been granted a free pass to come and go at any time I wish. But every time I come, I am to pay my respects to him, in other words he wants to see me, when I come to town." Explained Captain Moore.

Both men smile at what Captain Moore said.

The next day we received word that the emperor would see both of us.

The messengers stepped aside and bowed slightly. Then he singled, and Captain Moore, and General Scott were given two horses, they were made available by the samurai who was having trouble with them.

The horses that the two men have are a little high spirit. Samuel played a joke on us, but it backfired when Captain Moore and Scott were able to manage the horse with great skill.

We started our journey through the city. I notice how clean it is. The people stop what they were doing and bow from the waist, sometimes they kneel and lower their heads to show respect as we pass.

I glanced at the samurai that was escorting us, he did not return the bow instead he kept his eyes straight ahead.

Scott asks, "why are they doing that?"

"Doing What" Replied Captain Moore.

"The people are bowing as we pass, why." Ask Scott.

Captain Moore reminds Scott, "Do you remember what I told you aboard ship, how polit the people are showing respect to the samurai."

"I see, however there is one that didn't bow, she is just starring at us." Said Scott.

"Don't bring attention to anything we will talk when we are along." Said Captain Moore.

After, we said nothing for the rest of the ride.

Captain Moore noticed Scott kept looking around.

"Is something troubling you, my friend?" Ask Captain Moore.

"Hmmm Something is not right." Said Scott.

"And what will that be my young friend?" Captain Moore said. Scott said very seriously, "We are being watch."

Scott Motion with his head in the direction to his left where he saw the person, and at the same time said.

"Over there beside the…. Scott pauses, he has gone."

"How did you pick out one person from everyone around hear that is watching us?" Said Captain Moore.

"That person is the only one that was staring at us, and he did not bow. I also notice the same person at the docks. I did not say anything because I was not aware of the custom. Be size the samurai notice it too. When they approach the person, he seems to disappear before they got to him." Scott explained.

In a deep voice Captain Moore said, "Do not speck of this to anyone."

Both men became quit, doing the rest of the ride, but did pay more attention to their surroundings.

The Samurais escorted Captain Moore and Scott to a nice house near to the Emperor's Palace.

Captain Moore looks at the Samurai that were in charge and said in a strong voice, "We are here to see the emperor today."

The samurai looked at them with a smile and said, "Not today, today you will eat, food will be broth to you, you will also take a bath. Geisha girls will be available for you, compliment of the emperor, and tomorrow the emperor will see you. Our Emperor will have a feast in your honor, then he will listen to what you have to say." Explain the Samurai.

After Captain Moore translated what the Samurai had said. Scott bowed and replied, "tell the emperor thank you, but no thanks for the women I will have to prepare for our meeting.

Captain Moore turned to the Samurai and said something that made the Samurai smile and bow. Scott also bows and said, "Captain Moore, which went well."

Captain Moore remined Scott, "it will be an insult to refuse a gift from the emperor, and we do not want to insult the emperor, but do not you worry, my friend, you just get ready to see the Emperor and I will handle the four women. Captain Moore smile and said, the things I do for my country."

Both men bow at the Samurai. The Samurai secured Scott, and Moor horses and then Slowly rode off.

Captain Moore and Scott went into the house the emperor provided.

The house was small with two bedrooms. The emperor provided servants for the two men comfort. The servant picks the men bags up and went into the house. They followed their bags to their respected rooms.

Inside the room there was a tub of hot soapy water, and a geisha girl waiting. The servants put down their bags, bow and left.

The geisha woman took Scott by the hand and walk him over to the tub, then she started to undress him.

Scott did not protest in any way; he just believed that this was their custom. The geisha woman completely undressed Scott and guided him into the tub where she began to give him his bath.

After the woman has wash Scott, she dried him off, and put a robe on him, then she led him to the door and motion Scott to enter the main room. Captain Moore entered the room at the same time, the servants fixed them food and drinks. The woman took Scott by the hand and led him to the table, she sat him down and prepared his food.

Both men smile at each other. Captain Moore broke the silence and said, "Have you thought of what you are going to say to the emperor tomorrow?"

"I am going to use the direct approach." Answer Scott.

Captain Moore became serious and said, "That could work because they are a very direct people. But since you are new that will get us, both killed. Here is how you should address the emperor. Frist, when you are being introduce, you should get on your knees, lower your head, and tell him you have a gift from Emperor Washington, something that know other have in this area.

Then you swell his head with the praised. For example, you say, I came to you lord Emperor, because you are the only one that can grant for what I came to this land.

As you are aware, there are no greater worries though out the world greater than your Samurai, and none greater than the emperor who leads them.

Now say all this while you are on your knees. And make it sound like you mean it. Do not get up until the emperor tells you."

Scott replied, "got it, in fact I will use those very words."

Both men ate some more, then Scott said, "are the Samurai hard on the people for taxes?"

Captain Moore replied, "the people don't pay taxes."

"How does the army stay fed and clothed?" Said Scott.

Captain Moore explains, "the Samurai do not really need money, when they need something, it is given to them, by the people, food, clothes, horses, and a place to stay, anything they need. They very rarely traveled outside of their county, but sometimes they do, and only then they will carry money, lots of it, when they do leave, they look to better their way of life."

"Have the Samurai ever been robbed?" Scott Ask.

Captain Moore stretches his long legs out as he laid on his side, of the table, with a big smile he said, "There have been a few attempts, but you have to be out of your mind to rob a Samurai."

Their meal was interrupted when there was a knock on the door. Scott and Captain Moore looked at each other, they were not expecting anyone else. The men grab their pistols, Captain Moore walk to the door and slowly open it, so he could see who is there. He looked at Scott with a smile, then opened the door all the way, there were two more geisha girls standing in the doorway. Captain Moore motioned them to come in.

Captain Moore translated what the women said. "Therese two woman will clean up, and warm our beds for us, so it will not be cold when we turn in."

Scott remined Captain Moore, "what I thought you were going to take both woman?"

Captain Moore still smiling said, "I just said that so to get a reaction from you, but if the women are not found in your bed in the morning they will be put to death, understand this is a gift from the emperor, and specking of gift, have you thought of any?"

Scott became confused, "no, I aaa… haven't given it a thought."

Captain Moore said, "I got you cover in that department, don't worry about that."

Then Captain Moore put his arms around one of the women and walk to his room.

The women that were left with me is beautiful, she has long leg, shapely body, her eyes investigate your heart. Her lips were red as a rose and inviting. I was hypnotized by her beauty. I could do nothing but smile at her, but she did not return my smile and I started to feel uneasy. And that is when it happens, she looks at me and said in perfect English. "What are you doing here?" She said, "I was shocked and did not say a word. She became concerned that I did not understand what she was saying or that I was unable to understand her. So, she took a couple steps toward me and asked again.

She frowns and says, "I said what is it you want here; can you understand me?"

That snap me out of my trance.

"Yes! Yes, I can understand you." Said Scott.

"Then please tell me, what I want to know." She asks.

I do not know why, but I told her everything.

She said, "You will not get what you want from the emperor."

I was beginning to thank that there is something more to this woman than being a geisha.

With a strong voice Scott told her. "I didn't come all this way to be sent away empty handed."

She ignored what I was saying and went on to say. "After you meet with the emperor, and he refuse your request, you will be contacted."

"By whom?" Ask Scott."

She responded by saying, "The less you know the better you will be."

After hearing what she said, I knew I had to focus on my speech to the emperor. This may change a lot of things. So, I must make my speech in a way that will get my point across.

Scott told her, "I must attend to my speech for tomorrow."

"Do what you need to do, in the meantime I will go and warm your bed for you." She said. She turns, and as she walks toward my bedroom, she disrobes as she walks through the door and slips between the silk sheets.

I could not tear my eyes away from her, she is the most beautiful woman I have seen in my life.

That is when this feeling came over me for the first time benign in this country. She brought these feelings out of me. I had not felt this way since I was with Koko.

I must know her! I must! She must know what I was thanking because she said. "If you are finish with your speech, come to bed." She said it with a smile.

My answer was, "what speech?" I said as I started toward her.

When I got in bed with her, I had to ask. "What is your name?"

She put her hand on the left side of my neck and said, "Sylvia."

That is the last thing I remember until I woke up in the morning.

The next day someone came into my room, it was a Samurai with Captain Moore behind him with the three women flowing.

The Samurai looked at me and said something in his language, Captain Moore translated. "He wants to know where is the other woman that supposed to be with you?"

Before I could answer, a woman came out from under the sheets.

The Samurai looked at me and nodded his head.

He said something else to Captain Moore then left. Captain Moore walks the Samurai to the door while talking with him, when they reach the door Captain Moore bow and shut the door behind him. He turned and walked into my room and said, "We will meet with the emperor this evening. You save that woman life by not sending her away,' said Captain Moore.

Scott was staring at Captain Moore and said, "Except for one thing."

"And what is that?" Ask the Captain.

Scott looked at the door then back at Captain Moore and said, "She was not the same women I went to bed with last night."

Captain Moore turns to the woman and with a strong voice said. "Who are you, and where is the other woman?"

The woman fell to her knees and said in her language. "Please do not say anything to the Samurai. Sylvia will contact you."

Captain Moore translated what she said. Then he asks, 'Who is Sylvia. Scott looks at the woman and saw that she is worried of what I may say.

"Let her know, that we will not tell anyone. Her secret is safe with us." Said Scott.

Scott was wondering, and said aloud "Where is Sylvia?" Captain Moore translated.

The woman said, "all will be revel to you soon. I must go now."

Captain Moore looks puzzled. "What was that all about?" He asks.

"I don't know, but I don't think we are going to get what we need from the emperor," said Scott.

Captain Moore with a frown on his face look at Scott and said, "What did you mean, and why did you say that?"

Scott walks over to his bed and sits down; he looks up at Captain Moore and said, "Last night an Angel told me we will not get what we came for."

Captain Moore looks surprised. "A what!" Said Captain Moore.

Scott said, "The other woman that you left me with last night. Her name is Sylvia. WOW! What are we going to do?"

"I do not know but, play along like nothing happen we are going to ask the emperor for his help. We will stay with the mission." Said Captain Moore.

Scott asks, "what is the gift you have for me to give to the emperor?"

Captain Moore answer, "knowledge."

Scott looks at him confused. "What knowledge."

Captain Moore grabs a chair and moves it to Scott's side as if someone were listening. He said in a deep muffled voice.

"To improve their ships. I can make them more seaworthy, and the knowledge of how to build and sail it."

"What if the emperor refuses my request?" said Scott.

Captain Moore explains, "if he refuses, we will tell him that the ship is being built he will get it any way after we used it in our war. The Samurai can come back with us to keep an eye on the emperor's prize. If the ship is lost during the war. We will build another ship for you, even if we do not get what we want, we can keep negotiations open."

Scott returns his attention to his work, on his presentations the rest of the day.

Later that evening, before anyone could say another word the door opened and a Samurai was standing in the doorway, he said something, and Captain Moore translated.

"It is time."

Captain Moore told the Samurai we were ready. We walked out of the house with the Samurai leading the way. Captain Moore and I mounted our horses and went to meet the emperor. I went over a lot of things with Captain Moore on our way to the place. Things I needed to know in the meeting with the emperor.

CHAPTER 11

The Emperor

There is something else that was occupying my mind. I could not stop thinking about Sylvia. I could not see how she got out of my bed, and the other woman got in without me knowing.

"How did they do that?" I was not aware that I said that aloud. It got Captain Moore attention.

"You are thinking about her, the woman, aren't you?" He said, Scott answered, "Yes, it was something about her."

"I been thinking about what you told me, and something came to mind." Said Captain Moore.

"And what could that be "Ask Scott.

"It is best I tell you after we talk to the emperor when we are alone. If it is what I thank, we both could get killed just by saying their name." Said Captain Moore.

I was wondering what Captain Moore was thanking, but I decided to say nothing about Sylvia until we were alone. After that nothing else was said. We road though the place grate and dismounted. There were a lot of steps that led to a large door that opened into a courtyard. I looked around and was amazed.

"WOW! This is a big building; is this where the emperor works? Ask Scott.

Captain Moore smile and said, "No, this is where the emperor lives."

"This is his home?" Scott was surprised.

Captain Moore answer, "Why yes, yes, it is."

We walk up a long staircase. There was a guard on each step, and there were a lot of steps. We got to the top and stood in front of two huge doors with two guards on each side.

Captain Moore looks at me with a serious look and said, "ready or not here we go."

He nodded at the Samurai who was escorting us and said something to him. The guard nodded back then opened the huge doors. Captain More said, "Prepare to be amazed."

I was expecting to walk into a large room with the emperor sitting behind a large desk with a few of his aids standing beside him. What I saw was unbelievable, the room was so big you could put the Monika in it. His General's was sitting on each side of the runway.

Behind each General hung a banner that represent the regiment that is under his command, the closer I get to the Emperor the Higher the General rank. At the end of the runway there sat the number one General. They call him Shogun.

After the Shogun there are two steps, at the top of the steps was a platform with a man sitting in what looks like a chair with short legs and no back. This is where the emperor sits.

The runway itself was a long red carpet.

We walk halfway on the carpet when Captain Moore jester to stop and kneel on both knees, I did what Jeffery did and put my head on the floor.

Some of the General seem to look though us, and others nodded their heads in approval. We did not say a word until the emperor spoke first.

I found out later that the emperor said.

"It is good to see you my friend, have you decided to except my offer to stay in my Country?"

Captain Moore told the emperor, "Not yet there is trouble in my Country, and I am needed there. War is about to start. Which is why we are here."

The emperor said something and looked in my direction.

Captain Moore looked at me and said, "Your turn."

I remember what Captain Moore told me how to address the emperor.

I started out by saying, "Lord Emperor, Frist I must say I am amaze at your Country and the longer I stay here, I can see why Captain Moore speaks so highly of you, your worries, and your country.

Lord Emperor My name is General Scott Martin, and I am considered one of the best worries of my Country. I have no fear when I go into battle. My enemies that know of me fear me, that is, the ones that are still alive, but what I have seen since I've stepped foot in your magnificent Country, the only thing I can say, I am impressed and feel very humble in your presents.

My Emperor, George Washington sent me to ask you for your help in training our men for the upcoming war that Captain Moore spoke about.

My Emperor wishes to ask with the highest respect to bring back a few of your worries, to train our men."

Captain Moore has been translating everything I say. After I mentioned. To train our men. There was a low mummer in the room. All the Emperor's Generals are talking to each other. One of them had a concerned look on his face. It was the Shogun who asks a question, "Are you saying your Emperor want us to teach your people the way of the Samurai?"

Captain Moore translated what the Shogun said.

Scott told Captain Moore. "No sir, what I am asking for, is training in discipline, fitness, and a lot of hand-to-hand combat."

After Captain Moore translated, then there was more mummering.

The Shogun said something, and Captain Moore translated.

"And what do you have in return?" Said the Shogun.

Scott said, "as magnificent as your army is, your navy can be improved. We will offer you a war ship and the knowledge of building others.

There are war ships being built now. We will be happy to give you a ship in return. But first we will use it in the war, and if the ship is lost, we will build another one to give to you."

The emperor said something to Captain Moore, and Captain Moore translated it to me.

"We would like two ships."

Scott knew that the emperor was testing him.

Scott replied, "the emperor is wise, two is better. We also will teach your people how to build them.

The emperor said, "Give us two days to make this decision, and we will have an answer in the meantime enjoy your stay here in my country as my guess."

I ask Captain Moore, "translate something else."

"You're pushing it." Said Captain Moore.

"I have an idea." Said Scott.

"Okay, it is your head." Said Captain Moore.

"There is one more thing, may I have the horror of talking to one of your General's?" Ask Scott.

Captain Moore translates to the emperor what Scott said.

This surprised everyone in the hall.

"Why?" asked the emperor.

Scott reply, "In my Country this is a high horror, to sit down, have a drink, and talk to someone of equal rank."

The emperor responded, "What would you talk about?"

"Anything, and everything. We will talk about our country, battles we were in, our way of life, our personal family, our army's, everything." Scott said.

"We will see," said the emperor.

Scott and Captain Moore stood up, bowed, back up a few steps, bow again, turn and walk away.

As we were walking out, I could not help feeling we are being watch again I look around and saw her, the same women I saw yesterday at the docks, at the gates of the palaces, she was the one asking me question.

Sylvia.

Captain Moore must have read my mind.

"You don't have to say anything this time I see her too." Said Captain Moore.

"Do you know her?" Ask Scott.

"No, but I will inform the Samurai," said Captain Moore.

"No, she has something valuable to tell us. She will contact us soon enough. Then we will learn her intentions." Said Scott.

Captain Moore just shrugged his shoulders.

Scott smile and said, "in the meantime we are going to have some fun."

We went back to our rooms to prepare to see what life is all about here in this land after the sun goes down.

I was hoping to see Sylvia.

A few hours later I got dressed and was ready to go out to have a close look at the village.

Then there was a knock at the door. Captain Moore came out of his room with his pistol in one hand and a knife in the other. I walked to the door and asked. "Who is it?"

"I have a message from General Hi." Said the voice.

Scott said, "Wait I know that voice it's her." When I opened the door, I was pleased to see Sylvia.

"I am happy to see you again." Said Scott.

Surprised at what Scott said, Sylvia asks. Why?"

"Because, since I met you, I could not stop thinking about you." Said Scott.

Sylvia bows slightly at the waist and said, "I am very honored?"

Scott asks Sylvia, "why are you here?"

"I have a massage from General Hi," said Sylvia.

"Do you work for General Hi?" Scott said wondering.

Sylvia answered. "No, he does not waste his time looking at me. The women in this country are treated as a lower class according to the men, which is why the men could not tell one woman from the other.

However, General Hi is an honorable and good man. He has except your offer to dine with him.

"Okay Now we are getting somewhere. We are having dinner with one of the General." Said Scott looking at Captain Moore.

Sylvia put her hand on Scott's chest and said, "No! He only invited you."

Scott looks surprised, "Me! How will we understand each other?"

"You will find away." Said Sylvia.

"General Hi is a very intelligent man, it won't be hard," said Sylvia.

Captain Moore interrupted the two.

"General Hi is not just any General, he is Shogun. A powerful man. He answers only to the emperor and the other Generals answer only to him. He would be your best shot to get what you want." Said Captain Moore.

Scott asks Sylvia, "Do I have any hope in getting what I want?"

Sylvia said in a low and sad voice. "No, but what you said about the ships got them talking. They know the ones they have are not particularly good, they do need better ships to protect our shore's."

Scott looked at Sylvia hard and said, "You seem to know a lot about our business?"

Sylvia smiled and said, "I was there when you made your speech. Do not you remember, I made myself known to you."

"I do remember." Said Scott.

Captain Moore asks, "So, are you a Ninja?"

Before Sylvia could say anything, Scott butted in.

"All of this we are going to keep to ourselves. Captain Moore does not say anything to anybody. We will talk when I get back." Said Scott. Captain Moore looks at Scott a little worried.

"Be careful General Scott, Ninja aren't to be trusted," said Captain Moore as he looked at Sylvia hard without blinking.

"I think I am in good hands." Said Scott looking at Sylvia.

Sylvia smiles at Scott as they walk toward the carriage.

The carriage was private, with a door on each side. A man on top in the front that is the driver, one horse was all it took to drive the carriage, it was designed for privacy.

Sylvia and Scott climb aboard the carriage, Sylvia said something to the driver, and off they went to General Hi house.

On the way, Sylvia informs Scott on how to act in the General house.

When we arrive, a guard will escort you in.

I turn to say something to Sylvia and …. Scott purse…. She was not there, she just disappeared.

As I walk inside, I remember what Sylvia said, to bow and the General will bow in return, and not to sit until the General asks me to, and be polite, and everything will be all right.

When I walked into the General's house, I was alone at first. Then General Hi walked in the room, I bowed as instructed by Sylvia. The General bowed back. Then to my surprise General Spoke in English, "Please sit." General Hi said.

"You speak English?" Said Scott in amazement.

The General said, "yes I do."

He held out his hand for Scott to sit down.

"Please sit." Said General Hi again.

As I sat down, I said, "your people continue to empress me." The General bowed to accept the compliment.

Scott said, "I have to ask, where did you learned to speak English?"

"From your Captain Moore. Captain Moore has the respect of our Emperor. We are aware of people may come here from other counties around the world. So, we needed someone to understand your language. We cannot keep calling on Captain Moore to translate everything that is said. Bye the way your speech today was sincere respectful, and I felt you men's what you were saying, which tells us you are an honorable man" said General Hi.

Scott was happy to hear that, so he asked. "So, the Emperor will grant my request?"

"No, he will not." Said General Hi.

Scott looks surprised.

"Why not," asks Scott.

At first the General did not say anything. What he did was clap his hand and two women came in with food and sickie, the women put a plat in front of the two men. The other woman put a small cup in front of Scott, he looks into her eyes, and recognized her, it was Sylvia, but the only thing Scott said was, "Thank you."

"We have no desire to go beyond our borders, but we know we have a lot to offer other countries, however, we know we are going to need a Navy to protect us. Your gift to the emperors is most generous. However, we are a nation of warriors we do not wish to teach a potential future threat. I am sorry we must keep our battle strategies to ourselves. I am sorry for your country, but if it means anything, I was hoping you would get what you wanted but our Emperor said, "no" said General Hi.

Scott is saddened by the answer. Then he asks. "Will you send at least one person back with us to keep an eye on the emperors gift?"

General Hi smile and said, "you are also a very clever man General Scott, we felt you will ask us that question, and our answer is we already have two people who we trust looking out for the emperors grift. You and Captain Moore."

"The Emperor and his Generals are very wise," said Scott.

Although General Hi knew the answer to his next question he let him ask any way.

"We have denied your request, and you would still give us this gift?" Ask General Hi.

Scott answered, "yes, because you ask a friend a favor, and that friend said, no. That does not mean you are not my friend anymore. We still would like your friendship, and yes, we will still give you the ships, and all of what I said, after I have given my word, we continue talking about my country and many things is general.

Before I left General Hi gave me a scroll.

"What is this for?" ask Scott.

"Give this to the woman who brought you here." Said General Hi.

Scott bowed and left his House wondering what was in the scroll, he walked through the General courtyard thanking about all about what they were talking. When Scott approaches his carriage, the driver opens the door then bow, I return the bow and step inside, to Scott surprise. Sylvia was waiting for me.

"You are full of surprise." Said Scott.

Sylvia replied, "There more surprise to come."

"General Hi told me to give this to you." He said.

Once I gave the scroll to her, Sylvia took one look at it and put it aside.

"Are you going to open it?" Ask Scott.

"It is not for me." Said Sylvia.

Scott was confused and had to ask. "Who is it for?"

"It is for my master, the person who taught me everything he knows," she said,

"Please, tell me what it is you know; how do you get in and out of places without anyone seeing you? Who are you, what are you?" Ask Scott.

Sylvia smiled as she looked deep into Scott's eyes and said, "Who I am is Sylvia, What I am is…pause… the smile on her face went away, then she said. "Ninja."

Scott looks at her and said, "What is a Ninja?"

"You will know soon enough; however, I can say, it is all your wishes come true," said Sylvia.

Scott could not understand what she meant by that statement.

"My what?" said Scott.

Sylvia said, "I will tell you later, this is where I get off."

Sylvia leans close to Scott and kisses him passioned on the mouth and said, "I will see you later." She said.

The next thing I knew the driver woke me up and said, "we are here."

Captain Moore came out of the cottage to the carriage. Scott was a little daze, he looks around and said, "where are we?"

The driver answer, "you are at your cottage."

"When did the women get out?" ask Scott.

The driver looks at Scott oddly and said, "What woman? There were no one in the carriage but you."

Captain Moore did the translate between the two men. Scott looks a little disoriented, So, Captain Moore helps Scott out of the carriage.

"How does she do that?" Scott said not to talk to anyone. As they were entering the cottage.

Captain Moore asks, "why are you smiling, are we going to get what we want?"

"No, they are going to turn us down," said Scott.

"Then why are you so happy?" Ask Captain Moore.

"Because I saw her again, and this time she kisses me." Said Scott.

Captain Moore said angrily, "She kissed you! She kisses you! CAN SHE GIVE US WHAT WE WANT?"

Scott looks at Captain Moore with a big smile and said, "I think so."

Captain Moore was surprised and confused at the answer. "What! I never believe that the emperor would do that?" Captain Moore said.

"She does things that are unbelievable," said Scott with a serious look on his face.

"Stick to the subject. Did the General tell you that he is sending some Samurai with us?" Ask Captain Moore in a confusing way.

Captain Moore wanted some facts, "How are we getting what we want, who is this person you're talking about, and what unbelievable thing is this person doing?"

Scott with his head clearing, looked at Captain Moore and said, "Come inside I will tell you everything."

Scott and Captain Moore dismissed the driver and went inside. Both men sat down at a table and order some sickie. It was not until the two men has eaten and the servant clear their left-over food and was dismiss when the two men was free to speak of what happen.

Captain Moore straightens his legs out, adjust his pillows he was sitting on and said, "okay I have been very patient, I want to know everything?"

Scott smile and chuckle and began to tell Captain Moore what happen, to, at, and from General Hi home.

Captain Moore paused and began to worry.

"Ninjas are unwelcome news among the Samurai. You can have your head cut off just by saying the name Ninja.

Scott told Captain Moore, "She has been watching us ever since we arrived here. She was at the docks, when we went to the Palace, she was there.

She is the one that somehow knocks me out. The woman was at General Hi house, and she was with me here in the carriage, even though the driver told me different. She called herself a Ninja whatever that is."

Captain Moore face change, the blood just drains out of his face. He appeared to age before Scott eyes.

"What is the problem?" Said Scott.

Captain Moore looked nervous, he got close to Scott as if someone were listening, he tried his best to talk in a low calm voice.

"Ninjas are assassins for hire, although this one is acting very strange. They are something you do not want to deal with."

Captain Moore got even closer to Scott and said, "Their main weapon is to be able to move around people without beaning seen."

Therefore, your driver said he did not see anyone in your carriage, and if you see her in the palace, and the Samurai did not. She must be good; I did not know any Ninja was able to do that."

"There is more," said Scott.

Captain Moore stood up and said, "What could be more than what you just told me?"

Scott looks away and then looks back at Captain Moore and said, "I am in love with her, and I am sure that General Hi may have something to do with a Ninja."

Captain Moore was quiet for a moment, it seemed like hours; you can see the worry in his face.

"Scott be careful the Ninja always have a hidden agenda. Just be careful."

Said Captain Moore.

Scott smile and said, "don't worry my friend I'll be okay."

The concern was still in Captain Moore face. He asks Scott. "How are we going to get everything we ask for, if you already know that the emperor is going to say NO?"

Scott replied, "The scrolls I gave her may have something to do with it. What ever happen, it will happen after the meeting with the emperor."

Scott and Captain Moore did not say much to each other after that, they just said good night and went to bed with their separate thoughts.

The next day, I was prepared for rejection by the emperor, and this time I knew what to say to him. We are ready.

On the way to the palace Captain Moore was still concerned about the talk we had last night. He broke the silence by saying.

"I cannot help but to be afraid for you, my friend. The Ninja is nothing to trifle with, when you have this meeting with whoever, be careful. If you are not back by dawn. "I have no choice but to go to the emperor, and tell him what has transpired, said a concerned, Captain Moore.

Scott told his friend, "I understand, you do what you must, but I don't think it will come to that."

Captain Moore added, "I hope not, for your safety."

Nothing else was said until we were approaching the doors where the Emperor and his Generals were waiting.

Captain Moore asks Scott, "are you ready?"

Scott replied, "Oh yeah."

"Here we go." Said Captain Moore.

As before, we walked in, bowed, and again the emperor spoke first.

"Good morning to you General Scott and, to you Jeffery. I hope you slept well, and did you enjoy your visited with General Hi last night?" Ask the Emperor.

Scott replied "Good morning to you, your Highness, I hope you slept good as well, and good morning to you Gentleman, looking in the direction of the Generals. Yes sir, your highness, I slept very well. My talk with General Hi was very delightful, I learned about a lot of your life here. I am amazed everyday about your wonderful country."

The emperor smiled and said, "thank you, we have learned a lot from Captain Moore and yourself about your country. If the representatives are as respectful as you and Captain Moore, we welcome them."

"Thank you, sir that will go in my report, to my Emperor." Said Scott.

I began to think to myself as I looked at Captain Moore, I could tell by the look on his face he was thinking of something, what? I do not know.

Something happened after I left General HI's house, the emperor changed his mind, and is going to give me what I ask for.

Then the word came that kill our hopes.

"However, considering what we talked about yesterday. We are very protective of our way of life, although we invite your government to our shores. We do not venture out to other Countries because we are happy with what we have." Explain the Emperor.

"With all due respect your highness, by reaching out to other countries can only improve your way of life." Said Scott.

"You make a very good point but understand that we are very happy the way things are, the grift to the emperors is very generous, and it will fit our Navy well, so my Admirals have told me." The emperor explains.

Scott tried another attempt to convince the emperor.

"Your Highness if I could speck to your Admirals and Generals maybe I can point out the benefits of my quest." Said Scott.

The emperor knew what Scott was about to say. The emperor immediately responded.

"Mr. Scott, I have come to this decision before you got here, and some agree with you, in fact half of my Generals agree with you but it was the other half of my Generals who convince me."

Scott feels that if he can speak to his Admirals, he could change their minds and he could get what he needs for his country.

Scott tried a third time, "Your Highness, I ask you again just give me a few moments with your admirals."

The emperor admires Scott determination.

"You have already spook to my top General last night, and on your behalf, he made some very good points." Said the Emperor.

Scott turned and met General Hi eyes, and he bowed slightly, I bowed my head and turned back to the emperor.

The emperor went on to say, "I am sorry for you and your Country, but what I have decided stands. If it means anything to you, if your worries are anything like yourself, your Country will be all right."

"Thank you for your kind words, it means more than you would know. The ship that I promise you will be delivered to you after the war." Said Scott.

"I thank you General Scott, I would like to make one request about that. Could Captain Moore and his men deliver the ships. We are familiar with them." Ask the Emperor.

"As you wish," Scott answered.

Both men, Scott and Moore bowing at the same time, turn and walk out Scott now is looking forward to his meeting with the Ninja.

On the way out of the Place, General Hi caught up with Scott and Captain Moore.

"I am sorry you did not get what you came here for. But you are not finish yet." Said General Hi.

Scott asks him, "Does it have anything to do with the scroll you gave me last night?"

General Hi smiled and said, "I don't know what you are talking about."

He then turns and walk away saying, "you have a good day."

Scott answer, "You too sir."

Captain Moore frown and said, "what was that all about?"

Scott told Captain Moore, "General Hi gave me a scroll. I told you this yesterday. I was to give it to Sylvia who keeps showing up every now and then. I thank General Hi is the one who is setting the meeting with the Ninja."

Captain Moore said, "That is impossible."

"Why?" ask Scott.

Captain Moore explains, "the Samurai look at the Ninja as a clan without honor. They hate the Ninja, and the Ninja hate the Samurai. If the Emperor thanks General Hi is associating himself with the Ninja, he will be put to death instantly and without honor. Be careful Scott even though you did not get what you came here for, you still have accomplished a lot of things, but, know this, if you are caught with a Ninja, you also will be put to death."

Captain Moore gave me something to think about as we went to our cottage.

Later that evening no one had contacted us yet. We waited a few more hours and still nothing, I became very impatient.

"I am not going to set around hoping someone will come, I am going for a walk. If they do not come, then so be it." Scott said angrily.

Captain Moore said, "and if someone come while you are out?"

"Then they would miss me." Said Scott.

Captain Moore gave Scott a warning.

"Be careful and be back by dawn."

"Will do," said Scott.

As Scott was walking though the village, he was thinking that walking helps clear his head. I put up a good fight to get what my Country wants. Okay, we do not need any outside help. My town did defeat the British, and that is without our young men. That is what I will tell General Washington that we do not need anyone's help. We can fight our own battles.

"Yael! That is what I will tell him." Scott was saying this aloud.

Scott did not realize he was speaking aloud until he noticed everyone was looking at him. He smiled and nodded his head and kept walking.

"They must thank that I am out of my mind talking to myself," said Scott in a faint voice about the village people.

Scott could not help but smile at what had just happened. After that he just let his mind wonder as he walks, but more under control. Scott noticed that the air smelled good like Jasmine, and theirs a light breeze that felt cool on Scott's arms, he started to feel better and more relaxed.

Then Scott turned a corner and Sylvia was standing in front of him.
"How the hell do you do that!" Demanded Scott.
Sylvia responded by saying, "Very well thank you, come with me."
Scott first looks around, then walks after her.

We did not walk far, just a few blocks then turned down a narrow side street, we walked halfway down until we came to a small house. Sylvia knocks on the door; an elderly woman slid the door open and step aside and bow. A voice from in the room said.

"Come in Mr. Scott." In English.

I took two steps in and saw an old man sitting on the floor behind a table. At first, he just looks familiar to Scott.

Then it hit him.

"You were at the docks along with Sylvia when we arrived, and at the Palace with her, pointing at Sylvia, just before we went inside. So, I finally get to meet you." Said Scott.

"Please sit down it appears we were destining to meet." Said the old man.

Scott was on his guard and said, "and why should I sit down after all you are Ninjas aren't you?"

"You are a wise man, Yes, I am Ninja." Said the old man. Scott, concern ask, "Why am I hear, and what do you want with me?" The old man looks at Scott, he was still smiling and said, "You are here as my guest; I can offer you what you want. I can give it all to you, so please sit down let me show you."

Scott pauses for a moment, then sat down across from the old man. Unsure of what was going on Scott got comfortable then he said. "I was told that Ninja can't be trusted."

The old man replied, "that will depend on what we are trusted with.

"What is your name?" ask Scott.

"It is enough just to know your name." said the old man.

"Why are we talking in circles, talk to me straight, what is it you want from me," demanded Scott.

The old man looks at Scott and smile again.

"I desirer nothing from you, it is what you want, and I can give it to you." Said the old man.

Scott chuckled and asked. "And tell me sir about how you can give me what I want."

The two men are interrupted when two elderly women walk in, the one that answer the door, and another carrying a tray with tea. She sat it down in front of the old man, bow and left.

The old man pours some tea for Scott, and then he pours himself some, it was not until he took a sip of his tea when he answers Scott.

"I can see to it that your men get the training, that they needed to help your country win the war, "he said.

Scott told the old man, "I promise the emperor two warships just to be turn down, and hear you are offering me what I came here for, and yet you ask for nothing? So, I must ask, what is it you really want? You are full of deceptions, for example, this house does not look like anyone has been living here, no plants, and no furniture just a table, a pot of tea, two cups, and you and me."

The old man ignored what Scott said, and instead said.

"If I give you what you want, you have to do a favor for me."

Scott remembers what Captain Moore said. "Hear it comes, Captain. Moore were right a hidden agender."

I started smiling when I ask the old man. "And what is that."

The old man replied, "You have to take my pupil back with you, she can do all what you ask for, and more."

Scott wonder, "Who is this person?" Said Scott.

The old man looks at Scott as if he should already know the answer to that question than he said. "Sylvia."

That is when Sylvia walks into the room. I looked at Sylvia, she met my eyes. For the first time I really looked at Sylvia, she stood 5ft. 6in. or 5ft. 7in. Then Scott said, "How could a woman this small, give me what I want?"

That is when she walks over to me. I started to laugh and stood up and told Sylvia, "I guess we suppose to fight now to prove what the old man said?" Said Scott. Then he laughs some more. The old man said, "Yes, you should defend yourself." Now Scott is ready laughing aloud.

Scott said, "Against her what can she do to me. I am taller, bigger, and stronger.

Just then Sylvia took a step forward. She took his hand, kissed it on the back, and then she tossed him across the room.

Scott got up slowly to face Sylvia and said something very stupid.

"How did you do that?"

Sylvia answer, "Like this."

Sylvia grabbed Scott by the arm so fast he did not have time to react, and she tossed Scott back across the other side of the room.

The old man said nothing, he just smiled and watched.

This time Scott struggled to get to his feet.

Scott said, "Whit! I was not ready."

Scott recalls what Bear Claw taught him; he stood up and got into a fighting stance.

Sylvia asks, "are you ready now?"

"Yes, I am ready," said Scott.

Scott took a swing at Sylvia's head, she ducks kick Scott in the stomach, when Scott bent over in pain, he looks up just in time to see her spin and kick Scott on the side of his face. That was the last thing he felt before everything went dark.

Water must have been thrown on me because when I awoke, I was drenched. My head started to clear, then I heard a familiar voice.

"Are you alright?" The voice said.

To my surprise, it was General Hi.

"Are you all, right? The General asked again.

"No, I just got beaten up by a small girl." Said Scott.

General Hi laugh.

"How can someone so small can be so deadly?" said Scott.

When Scott was saying this, General Hi was helping Scott to his feet.

General Hi explains, "It does not matter how tall or how small you are, with the right training you can always defeat your enemy. My friend, she is the one that can give you what you want."

"But I heard that Ninja can't be trusted?"

"What Ninja? You were only asked to fill the wishes of an old man." Said General Hi.

"But how am I going to leaved your country with one of your own people?" Scott asks.

General Hi look at me with a smile and said, "you will not."

He pointed at Sylvia and before my eyes she transforms from a Japanese woman to a Colonial by taken her make up off. Scott was in disbelief.

Scott asks, "how do you do that?"

Sylvia said. "You ask that a lot."

"I must confess I was going to ask you to come back with me anyway," said Scott.

Sylvia did not say a word, just smiled and stepped toward Scott and kissed him on the side of his face.

"Thank you for not knocking me out this time," Scott said gratefully.

General Hi walks to the door quietly, he is in a rush for this to end. "Sylvia will tell you her story later, now it is time I must go." Side General Hi.

Scott reassures General Hi, about the ships, "I will still honor my promise to your Emperor."

General Hi said, "Thank you, then he bows slightly."

Scott returns the bow, and that, is when he realizes that the old man is no longer here.

"Where is the old man?" Scott asks Sylvia.

"You will see him again later; for now, what he came here to do is to talk to you. I will meet you at the docks, do not leave without me." Said Sylvia, she blew, gave him a kiss, then stepped through the door and disappeared.

I am left in the cottage alone. I looked around and said aloud.

"Well, what the hell, why am I still standing here" I went to the Door look back and left.

When I got back to the cottage where he was staying just before dawn. Captain Moore was there, waiting for me, pacing back and forth.

When I came through the door, he walked over to Captain Moore. Before Scott could say anything, Captain Moore said.

"I stayed up all night wondering what happened to you. You are not doing my heart any good my boy. I started to thank you were dead. No one came to the meeting. What happen?"

Scott grabbed Captain Moore's arm in the bicep, looked him in the eyes and said, "We got what we came for."

Captain Moore was surprised. He pauses and says in a faint voice, "The emperor gave us what we wanted?"

"No, I will explain later, but we have to say our goodbyes and get to the docks and aboard ship, there we will get what we came for. Then we will get under way." Said Scott.

Captain Moore looked at me with one eye closed and said very worried. "You didn't do anything stupid did you?"

Scott smiled as he was getting his stuff together, he said. "No, and thanks for your conformance in me. We are going to have a passage." Captain Moore was amazed by what Scott said.

"Did you work a magical" asked Captain Moore.

Scott replied, "No, but God gave us one. We just need to get aboard the ship."

Captain Moore and Scott did not say another word, they rushed to get their stuff together, Scott left first with Captain Moore behind him. Captain Moore stops at the door to check the room to make sure there is nothing left.

The men mounted their horses and road though the village until they reach the docks.

Scott went aboard the ship first, while Captain Moore addressed the Samurai in charge.

Captain Moore bowed, and said to the Samurai, "Give the Emperor my apologies and let him know that I will see him when I come back with his ship. Tell the Emperor to stay safe, and healthy until my return."

Bout men bow, and Captain Moore boarded his ship. When he put his feet on Deck he yelled. "Prepare to get underway."

The first mate responded, "aye sir,"

He turned and faced the crew and repeated the captains' orders. "Prepare to get underway."

The crew rushed to their station.

Captain Moore joins Scott, who was looking at the docks.

"Okay, where is this magical?" Said Captain Moore.

Scott pointed to a big breast, and big behind woman, wearing long blue dress and a hat to match, the hat was moving loosely but somehow manages to stay on her head. The parcel she was carrying kept her in the shade and hiding her face from the samurai.

Captain Moore looks to see what Scott is pointing at and saw a woman with lots of luggage. She was fussing at everyone aloud. The two men watch the woman yelling at everybody.

She was telling the people that were overseeing her luggage, "Be careful with that! Do not you drop that, are you crazy I told you to keep that one level, can you people move any faster."

When she arrived at the ship she said, "OH MY GOD! What kind of boat is this? I hope it will not sink after we leave. Who is the captain on this, this boat?" She yells.

Sylvia was pretending to be someone that people would be glad to get rid of.

Her wig was crooked, she had too much make up on, a mole on her nose, and on her chin with one or two hairs coming out of it.

Her fingernails are long and broken. She was fat.

Even the Samurai pitched in to help with her stuff on board the ship, just to get rid of her.

Captain Moore became upset about her calling his ship a boat. "I am the Captain of the Monika it's my ship, and who are you?" Said Captain Moore.

"I am your passenger, which is all you need to know. Is this ship seaworthy?" Said the woman.

Captain Moore tries hard not to get angry.

"I beg your pardon mam this is one of the finest ships on the seas" Captain Moore said very proudly.

"OH MY GOD, I HATE TO SEE THE OTHER SHIPS!!! WHERE IS MY CABINET?" Yell the woman.

"Over there." Captain Moore pointed to the rear of the ship.

The woman looks at Captain Moore for a long time with her nose in the air saying. "Do you have a crew or are you going to take my bags to my cabin yourself?"

That was all Captain Moore could take. "I have had enough of you misses. I will tell you where you can take your bags." Said Captain Moore.

Before the captain could complete his sentence Scott interrupted him.

"I'll oversee the lady's bags just get underway." Said Scott.

"Well, at last there is one gentleman on this tub." Said the woman.

As the woman was walking to her cabin, she notices the crew staring at her.

The woman yelled at the crew. "WHAT ARE YOU MEN LOOKING AT? DON'T YOU HAVE SOMETHING TO DO? GET TO IT!"

Everyone started tripping over each other to get out of her way.

Once in the cabin, Scott and Sylvia turned to each other and laughed hard and loud.

Captain Moore was staring at the direction the woman and Scott went, when his first mate walks over to him and said, "This is going to be some trip."

Captain Moore replied, "Yes, it is. Take the Monika out sir."

The ship screech as it pulls away from the docks, slowly at first, then it picks up speed as the sails unfold. Scott came out of the cabin and walked over to Captain Moore.

It was an hour when Sylvia came out of her cabin, with a lovely dress on, and looking like her beautiful self. At first the crew was confused, because only two people went into the cabin, and she was not one of them. Then the crew started to understand with the help of the first mate. Sylvia walks on deck toward Scott and Captain Moore.

"Oh no hear comes that woman." Said Captain Moore.

CHAPTER 12

The Journey Back

Scott turned, and seeing Sylvia brought a smile to his face.

He informed Captain Moore, "Do not worry Captain, what you saw before at the docks was nothing but a show. It was stage, so she could get out of the country without question, as you can see, she is totally a different woman.

Captain Moore took a good look at Sylvia, and said, "Oh my I see what you mean, she is quite lovely."

Sylvia stood by Scott's side. The mole was gone off her nose, and chin, her wig was gone, and her makeup was a lot better. What stood beside Scott was one beautiful woman.

"I am so sorry Captain Moore if I cause you and your men any problems, "said Sylvia Apologetic.

Captain Moore pretended that it was not a problem at all. "I just wish our mission was a success," said Captain Moore.

"Oh, but it was better than I hoped for," said Scott.

What Scott just said put a frown on Captain Moore face.

"How so," ask Captain Moore.

Scott knew how Captain Moore would act when he here the news. "We have a Ninja to teach us." Said Scott.

Captain Moore got really concerned, he stood there looking around expecting to see something.

He turns to Scott with Sylvia standing right beside him and said in a faint voice. "You mean to tell me a Ninja gotten aboard my ship without me knowing it?"

Scott replied, "Oh, but you knew it in fact the whole crew knew it."

"I don't recall seeing anyone, where is he?" Said Captain Moore.

"The Ninjas is not he. The Ninja is she, and she is standing in front of you." Said Scott with a big smile.

Captain Moore looks at Sylvia in shock.

"No, no, no, no! You mean to tell me that she is a Ninja? Side Captain Moore, surprisingly.

Sylvia held out her hand and said, "glade to meet you, Captain."

Captain Moore kisses the back of her hand as they walk to his cabin. Scott closes the door behind him and sat down with Sylvia across Captain Moore desk.

It was hard for Captain Moore to understand. He sat down behind his desk, opened a drawer, and pulled out a bottle of rum, and said, "Drink up, we are celebrating. We got what we wanted."

CHAPTER 13

Back at the Campfire

Everyone around the campfire was focused on Scott telling his story.

Sylvia added, "I did not know that was the start of The Five at the time."

"Yes, it was, it also was the start of me giving my heart to someone for the second time in my life," said Scott.

Someone ask, "What happen to Captain Moore?"

"Captain Moore had more adventures after that. Before he joined the Five and before he was put in charge of our Navy. Which I will tell you about at a different time," said Scott.

"After the war we kept our word to the Emperor of Japan, and delivered two ships to him, and that is where Captain Moore lives for a while.

When Scott first started his story, he had some people listening to him. Now that he has finished with his version of The Five. There was a large audience of people still coming to sit down and listen to how The Five begin.

Before Scott could continue, Wanda asks.

"Whit! Stop! Before you go any further, I would like to hear how you got to Japan Ms. Martin, and do not stop until you get on board the ship coming back."

All eyes turn to Sylvia and give her their undivided attention. Sylvia paused to gather her thoughts then she smiled and said,

Sylvia's Story

SYLVIA'S TABLE OF CONTENTS

The Voyage

My grandparents had a lot of money and told my parents not to follow everyone else's dream, but to pursue our own. This is a big world, and there is something out there waiting for you to discover, find your spot in it and grow from there.

My parents' names are Montgomery and Ellen Holmes. My mother told me she did not understand what my grandparents meant by that, but my father did. So, when the next ship was bound to the new world, we will be on it.

During the voyage to the new country, the trip was boring, but my parents did manage to find some excitement. My mother became pregnant.

When the ship docks in the new world they decide to go farther west. My parents had their sights set on going west, but my father was going to delay the trip because of my mother pregnancy, but my mother disagree, she said, "no, we will go as plan."

My father stands 5ft. 10in. and a bit overweight and is a very smart man. My mother said that is one of the things she loves about him. My father is also a stubborn man, but it was my mother that always get the last word. He looks after my mother and fusses over her a lot during his arrangement for us to move west. We carried a lot of gold coins with us, and my father only carried a small amount in his pockets. He needed it for the preparations for our journey. When things were ready, we headed West.

From what she told me. "There were about 20 to 30 people that decided to do the same as we did. We joined a wagon train.

The trip was slow but rewarding. My parents were getting acquainted with the rest of the people, they found that they were good company. The man who my father paid to take us West was a good man; he told my father that he has done this many times before, and that they know the terrain well. This is how they make their living. These men are paid enough money to pay for their trip to where we are going, and their trip back, and enough left over for supplies, and saving, then start all over again. And if they are lucky, they may have people that want to come back east. This will be a bonus to them.

The trip was going well, we saw some hostile Indians that we avoided and got help from others when we stop for supplies.

Two thirds of the way into the trip my mother was five months into her pregnancy with me. The wagon train came across a nice town, where we stopped to get supplies, and stayed a few days. During this time, my father decided to do some exploring.

The first night my parents went out to go looking around, they came across a cave with a man sitting at the mouth with a fire. The man looks tired, worn out beyond his years. He was a broken man who's only wish is to live out the rest of his years in peace.

My father approaches the man, and ask, "are you alright, do you need any help?"

The old man replied, "Maybe, who are you?"

CHAPTER 2

The Discovery

My name is Montgomery Holmes, this my wife Ellen we were out to look at your find country."

The old man said, "yes this is a find piece of land. That is why I purchased it. This is legally my land, and the open to this cave, is really the entrance to a silver mine. I have been hitting a few small veins that keep me in supplies, and food on my table, but never the mother vein. But now I am tired. I just wish to live in town comfortably. All I need is enough money for someone to buy my land, and I will be a happy man."

Montgomery said, "I never seen a Silver mine before, will you show it to me?"

The man said, "sure, come I'll give you the two-dollar tour."

The two men walk a few steps into the mine. The old man stops and says, "Really it's two dollars."

Montgomery smile and said, "I am sorry I thought you were kidding?"

The old man answer, "No I was not. I do not kid when it comes to money?"

Montgomery gave the old man two dollars and said, "Now, now about that tour."

The old man took the money put it in his pocket. After the tour, the two man was walking toward the exit the old man said, "you know I am a good judge of character and I can tell, you are a good man, so I will be straight with you. The mother vain is here it and it is close, but I cannot penpoint it. Now I am too old and too tired. You might be the one who can find it. I tell you what, I will sale it to you for ten thousand dollars, and I will even stay and help you get started, but as soon as you are settled, I am leaving okay?"

Montgomery looked around and said, "I don't have ten thousand dollars."

The old man body slumped, and he exhale loudly, he turns and said, "the exit is this way."

The old man took a few steps.

Then Montgomery said, "But I do have ten thousand dollars in Gold."

The old man stops in his tracks and with a big grin he said. "Did I tell you my name is Carlos, and I feel that this is the start of a beautiful friendship."

I am finding new energy toward the task of working the mine, he told Montgomery. "The first thing we need to do is get proper supplies.

Montgomery interrupted Carlos. "No, the first thing we have to do is to convince my wife that there is a delay in our travels."

Montgomery exits the mine with a big smile on his face. As he walks toward his wife. Before Montgomery could say a word. Ellen made up her mind to speak first.

"I already know you want to work this cave." Said Ellen.

Montgomery said, "it's called a mine."

"Don't interrupt." Ellen told her husband.

But Montgomery press on, "give me some time, I know this is not our destination, but I see this is an opportunity for us, I can't explain it, but I felt something when we entered the mine, we will move on at a later time."

"We will stay until I have had enough, then we will leave." Said Ellen.

"Yes dear." Said Montgomery.

Ellen continued, "You will build me a house, not a hut, a house. I will not stand for anything less. Do you understand that?" Montgomery said, "Yes dear."

"Good now let us go back to town so you can get some rest. And so, I can have our baby." Ellen Said.

For the third time Montgomery responded, "Yes dear."

As the two men walk around to the other side of the wagon. Carlos said. "Man, what a woman."

Montgomery said proudly, "Yes, what a woman."

Montgomery and Carlos climbed on the wagon and halfway into town, Ellen let out a loud yell. Both men look at her. Montgomery said, "What is it, Ellen?"

"The baby is coming," said Ellen.

Montgomery and Carlos helped Ellen in the back of the wagon, Montgomery climbed in the back with Ellen, and Carlos took control of the wagon, and yelled, with the snap of the whip. The horse rears up on its hind legs and started toward town at a full gallop, they did not stop until they arrived at the doctor's office.

Before long Mr. and Ms. Holmes were blessed with a baby girl.

Ellen said, "what do you think we should name her?"

"How about Silver, in horned of the mine." Said Montgomery.

Ellen said, "that sounds like something you name a horse, no. We will name her Sylvia." Said Ellen.

Montgomery like the sound of the name, "Sylvia it is." Montgomery said.

The next day Montgomery told the wagon Master, "there is a change in my plans, and we will not be continuing with you."

The wagon master said, "you are crazy to do this. There is no refund."

"Maybe I am, but it will eat at my gut if I did not. And about the refund, I understand. Said Holmes.

The following day, at noon Holmes, Carlos, and eight (8) other men, along with all the supplies they would need for now, to build a house, and a bunkhouse for the men.

"After the house and bunkhouse is build, we will go to the mine." Said Montgomery.

The house was a three-bedroom home with a dining room, kitchen, living room and a study where Montgomery does his paperwork.

The land has been renamed the Holmes estate.

The living quarters for the men was a three-room bunkhouse, a fireplace a large room where the men can get together comfortably, with two abjointing rooms were the men sleep. The men were grateful for what they have. The eight men Montgomery hired were men that had no place of their own, some sleep outside of stores to survive, some clean stable, run Aaron is, anything to make money to eat. So, what Montgomery offered was a step up.

What Montgomery offered them was a roof over their head, three meals a day, payment for working at the mine, plus three percent of the findings.

Once the house and bunkhouse are built their attention turns to mine. For a while everyone was excited, because every now and then the men will hit a small vain which helps put money in their pockets. It also kept their supplies updated.

Ellen has her job also; she kept the men fade clean the house and take care of Sylvia. The men say that Ellen work harder than anyone else.

It has been four months now, and the men found nothing. The last vain they hit played out six weeks ago.

Montgomery could see the men were getting frustrated, so, he gave them the week end off, and put extra money in their hands, to have a fun time in town.

Montgomery told his men, "I understand how you feel, and if you do not come back, I will understand that too.

One-man steps forward and said, "Mr. Holmes sir I speck for us all.

We thank you for all you have done for us, and we will see you Monday."

"Thank you, have a good time in town men." Said Montgomery.

Everyone went to town except Carlos.

"I am too old to carry on like some young Bull, I'm going to bed," said Carlos.

Montgomery watch as the men road off. The men were not the only one that was frustrated so was Montgomery. Doubt started to set in.

Montgomery walks back into the house and sits down at the table. His wife came over to him and said, "Sweetheart you and the men have been working hard in the mine for the past 21 months, it is good you gave them the weekend off, now you can relax and collect your though."

Ellen has always been loving and supportive of her husband, whatever he does was for the good of the family.

He has never disappointed his wife. Thinking to himself I will not disappoint her now.

Montgomery said, "thank you dear. That is exactly what I needed. I am going to go out to the mine and walk though just to see if I can start something new Monday."

"Okay honey, do not be too long: I will wait up." Said Ellen.

Montgomery finished his meal still in deep thought about what he could do different in the mine, he walked out of the house and sat on the front porch staring at the mouth of the mine.

Montgomery walks to the mine thinking to himself, "what am I missing? The mother vain is here, like the old man said, I can fill it."

Montgomery picks a pickax and walk into the mime and started to pick at the same place his men was digging. He found nothing. Frustration started to sit in again, this time Ellen was not around to calm him down.

Montgomery kept saying. "It's here, it's here I know it."

Frustration was building up inside of him until he exploded, and he threw his pickax to the side of the mine's wall where it stuck.

Montgomery, breathing heavily, he started to calm himself down a bit.

Now under control enough to go back to the house, and to the loving arms of his wife. That brought a smile to his face.

Montgomery went to the pickax, pulled it out of the wall, and saw something shiny where the pickax was.

Montgomery just chuckled and said to himself, "another vein, that is good at lease the men have something to come back to."

Montgomery chip at the new vain, and it kept getting wider, wider, and wider. He started to get excited, this vein was about two feet wide and ran along the wall of the mine.

At first Montgomery said in a low and disbelief voice. "It's been here all the time running along the side of the wall right next to us." Then he yielded as loud as he could. "YIPPEE, YIPPEE!!!

Montgomery yelled so loud, Ellen came out of the house looking at the mine thinking the worse, she ran toward it and met her husband as he came out.

"Montgomery what's wrong?" Ask Ellen.

Montgomery did not say anything at first, he just grabbed her and very passionately kissed her.

Ellen said, "Well I know there is nothing wrong. What got you in such a good mood suddenly?"

"I found it, I found it." Montgomery said.

"Found what?" said Ellen.

"The mother vain, it was right beside us all along." Said Montgomery.

Montgomery and Ellen were making so much noise that it brought out the only person that did not go to town. Carlos, the old man. "What the hell are you two carrying on about." Said Carlos.

Montgomery did not tell him why, he just said, "go to town and get the men, tell them something happen in the mine, and hurry."

The old man though the worse, he fears it was a cave in. All their work could be lost. Montgomery told Carlos to go in town and get the man. Carlos got in a wagon as fast as he could and drove to town.

In town the men were having a time of their life. They had money, drinks, and the woman were very friendly.

Carlos burst into the pub, sweat pouring from his face. The men that Carlos was looking for saw him come in and immediately invited him over to their table, he walks over to the table and in a faint voice said, "cave in."

All eight men stood up simultaneous they said nothing, they gup their drinks down and run out of the salon, jump in their wagons, and went to see how bad it is.

When the men got to the Holmes estate Montgomery and Ellen was sitting on the front porch in a rocking chair smiling.

One of the men ran to Montgomery and said, "what happen?"

Montgomery had a large box in front of him, he pushes the box toward the men and said, "Drink up boys we are rich." The men were confused.

Montgomery saw the confusion on their faces, so he made himself clear.

"I found the mother vein," Montgomery said.

One of the men said, "Great Mother of God, where was it?"

"It has been right alongside us all the time. If you trace the vein, it will lead you to the mother lode." Said Carlos.

Without another word the man ran to the mine. When they came out, they were screaming and yelling.

After the main vein had been discovered, we followed it to the treasure trove, just like Carlos said it would.

My father mines the silver for the next three years, it seems the more they dig the more silver they uncover.

My father is a very generous man, and true to his word, although he promises the men three percent it was still enough to make the men rich.

Carlos said that he did not want any part of it, but he did take enough of it to purchase the hotel in town. He lives there now, and that is where he will be for the remainder of his days.

My father had money in the bank back East, so, he had a great deal of his part of the sliver sent back there, with a simple phrase that only the bank president and himself knows, and only to be handed down to the next president if there is one. Who every comes to the bank with this phrase is the owner of the money? It was so much silver the bank president had to have an underground vault built.

My father hired more men to work the mine. The original eight men became supervisors, and some sat on the town board of trustees. Which consist of only the eight men. Carlos made sure my father shares got back East. The town grew fast and was renamed Carlos's city.

The Journey Continues

And as for my parents, one day my mother sat down with my father and said, "Sylvia is now three years old. I like to continue our journey."

Now that Montgomery has his own wealth and does not have to rely on the money that his father gave him when he left England. Montgomery is now ready to make the trip he started three years ago.

The town is a regular stop for wagon trains headed West. When we rejoin one of the wagon trains, we join it with a lot of money and silver coins.

Shortly after arriving in California my father decided to look at the largest ocean in the world. He was walking on the docks when he overheard two men talking, who the two men where, was unimportant, what they were talking about is.

The two men were talking about a place, unlike any other. A place that was self-sustained, and with no hard ship, a very peaceful place.

My father believed that sounded like a delightful place to raise a family. He approaches the two men and address them.

Montgomery said, "I am sorry to ease drop on you two good men, but I could not help but over here you two gentlemen talking about this place that you describe. Could you please tell me where it is and what is it called?"

"And who are you?" One-man answers suspiciously.

"My name is Montgomery Holmes, and I would like to know more about this place. I have been searching for such a place for a long time. So, could you please tell me where it is and what it is called?" Said Montgomery.

The man said, "I don't know much about the place, what I only know, is what my Captain tells me."

"And where can I find this Captain?" Ask Montgomery.

The man smiles and says, "Well you are in luck because he is standing right over there."

The man pointed to the captain who is bent over a barrow looking at some papers with a lantern being the only light to see by.

Montgomery looks to see who the man was pointing at, then he looks back at the man and said, "Thank you."

After Montgomery thank the man, he turns and walk over to the captain and introduce himself. "Pardon me Captain I am sorry to interrupt you; my name is Montgomery Holmes and I overheard two of your men talking about a place that you have describe as paradise. I understand that you know where and what it is. The two men inform me about it and said you are the one that knows all about it."

As Montgomery was specking, he pointed to the two men about whom he was talking.

The captain looks to see who Mr. Holmes was talking about. He saw the two men as they wave.

"Oh yes, I did talk to them about a place that fit that description. However, the people at this are strict about their rules, and they do not like outsiders. They also do not like change to their way of life." Said the Captain.

Montgomery was delighted in what the captain said "It sounds like a place I been looking for. I do not want to change anything. The way it sounds may be a wonderful place to raise a family. How much will you charge to take me and my family there?" Montgomery said.

The captain informs my father, "A trip like that will cost a plenty."

Montgomery reaches into his pouch and pulls a bag of silver coins and pushes it toward the captain.

"Will this be enough," said Montgomery.

The captain picks up the bag and looks inside, his eyes widened with a smile.

"My Lord, how many people are in your family?" Ask the Captain.

Montgomery smile and said, "Just me, my wife Ellen, and my daughter Sylvia."

"Sylvia, I never heard of a name like that before. Just how old is your daughter," said the captain.

"Three years old, why?" Montgomery asks suspiciously.

The captain notices angry in Montgomery voice.

"I do not mean any disrespect, but she is young to make a trip like this. We will be at sea for a long time. That could be hard on someone so young." The captain said.

Montgomery shook the captain's hand and said, "Do not concern yourself about her, after all she is a Holmes, and us Holmes come from good stock, by the way sir, what is your name?"

"Call me Captain Roberts." The captain said.

"Okay, Captain Robert it is, when can we be on our way?" Said Montgomery.

"We will leave in two days." Answer Captain Robert.

"We will be here in two days." Said my father excitedly.

Two days later that morning, Montgomery and his family show up on time, and ready to see their next wonder. We pulled away from the docks and sat out for the open sea not knowing what lies ahead.

CHAPTER 4

The Voyage to Paradise

We were at sea for a long time. We found out early in the trip that there was another family aboard. Their last name was Page, who had a little girl by the name of Margaret. She had long black hair with a blue bow in it, her dress was blue with white trim. We became good friends and since we are the only children aboard, we were together from sun-up to sundown.

The family is going to a place of beauty, there are islands that are very peaceful. The name of the place, I cannot remember what they call it.

What I do remember is it was beautiful. This is where my friend and her family are going.

When the time came to say goodbye, it was hard, you see she was the first friend I ever had. I did see her once more when we left Japan.

After about a week or so, we came across some rough waters with huge waves. The first mate told Mr. and Ms. Holmes to go back to their cabin and ride it out there. My mother looked around for me and could not find me anywhere.

Ellen became nervous, she did not know what had happened to me. My mother, father, and the crew looked for me throughout the ship and could not find me anywhere.

My mother became scared that I may have fallen overboard, my father was on the verge of panicked, my mother was becoming hysterical, everyone ran to the captain's Quarters, we bang on the door.

The captain said, "Who's at my door?"

My father replied. "Sir, I must speak to you on a matter of great important."

"Come in." Said Captain Roberts.

When my father entered, he saw me in the captain's lap looking at charts.

"Yes, what is it?" Said Captain Roberts.

Both the Captain and Sylvia were looking at Montgomery.

Montgomery was relieved to see that Sylvia was all right.

"Sir, I have come for Sylvia. The first mate orders us back to our cabin until the storm passes." Said Montgomery.

The captain looks at Sylvia and said, "after the sea has gotten better, with your father permission, have your father bring you back to my quarters, and I will finish teaching you about the charts, and how to navigate the waters." Said Captain Robert.

"Yes sir, I will ask my father if I can come back." Sylvia said.

Sylvia jumps off the captain's lap and runs to her father. Montgomery kissed and hugged her. They started to exit the captain's quarters, as Montgomery was leaving through the door, he looked over his shoulder and smiled, and nodded as if to say thank you. The captain returns the nod to say you're welcome without speaking.

My father, and I joined my mother, who were happy to see me, all three of us went back to our cabin and waited until the storm was over.

The seas were hard. waves were high, the wind rip the main sail, but the captain is a very experience man of the seas. He kept the ship afloat and on course, he fought for hours. After the storm was over with, everyone was able to calm down. The storm was scary, but we survived.

After a few days when the ocean clams down, my father kept his word and took me back to the captains' quarters, so she could continue her education on the charts.

Montgomery kisses me and says, "Behave yourself."

"Yes, daddy," said Sylvia.

Captain Roberts took me by the hand smile and said to my father, "Sylvia is in good hands."

Captain Robert and Sylvia walk over to his desk, he lifts Sylvia up on his knee and said, "Now, where were we?" The rest of the trip was very educational.

CHAPTER 5

Japan

When we reach Japan, it was like being in another world, everything was very stranger to us, my father informed me that this is the way people are in this land.

The people were small, with an oval face, and their eyes slanted, which gave them a nice and pleasant look.

I was three when I started this trip. I turn four years old doing the trip over here, and this is the only time I have been out of my country.

As our baggage was unloaded off the ship. I wandered off from my parents while they were talking, but not far.

As I walked, people were saying something to each other smiling and saying something to me. But I did not understand what they were saying. One woman offers me something, she jester me over to her, she seems like a nice woman, so I walk to her, she pointed to her own mouth and put something in it. She closes her eyes and makes a delicious sound. I laughed a little at her and she smiled back at me. The lady offers me some of whatever she has. It was about three inches long. I broke off a piece of it and put it in my mouth. There was a pause, then, I was in heaven. After I taste it, I said, "thank you."

I thank the lady understood what I said, because she smiled at Sylvia and nodded her head. I did not know why she took a couple steps backward and bowed at the waist. I do not know why I bowed to her as I was backing up, then I bumped into someone.

The person had his back to Sylvia, he turned quickly with his hand on his sword. At first, we both just looked at each other.

I smile at this man and say, "I am sorry sir if I frighten you, please accept my apology," said Sylvia.

The man was huge about 6ft. 1in a little taller than my father and fit. His hair was long in a ponytail just on his shoulders. He is extraordinarily strong. He has two swords on his waist, a long one on his left side and a short one on his right.

The man looks at Sylvia for what seems like an exceptionally long time and said, "You did not frighten me" in perfect English.

He looks important so I try to make friends with him.

Sylvia said, "Excuse me sir would you like a piece of my candy?"

He did not say a word; he just reached down, took the candy and bit it.

"Hmmm, this is incredibly good. Where did you get such a treat?" Ask the man.

Sylvia turned and pointed over to the woman, who gave me the treat.

We both walked over to the merchant. The merchant saw us coming and went to her knees and placed her head on the ground.

The man told her to stand, and he said, "I will have four treats of the same as you gave this child." He was talking in a different language.

The merchant gave the man the four treats and bowed, the man paid for it, turn away from the merchant toward Sylvia, he gave me two of them.

"Where are your parents?" Ask the man.

Sylvia turned around and pointed at her mother and father.

There was a woman that was helping my parents, she saw us approaching her eyes widen, you can easily see she was frighten out of her mine.

As Sylvia and the man got closer, I was feeling proud of myself for making a new friend.

The woman said something a loud, everyone on the docks turns toward us and bowed.

When we arrived, the woman did the same as the merchant did, she went to her knees and put her head on the ground, and so did everyone else on the docks.

My mother and father bowed full at the waist and said, "Good day sir." Montgomery said.

The man said. "Is this your daughter?"

"Yes sir, she is, I am sorry if she causes any trouble," apologize Montgomery.

The man just grunted and said, "She causes me no trouble; she is a very smart young lady. Tell me, who are you and why are you here?"

"My name is Montgomery Holmes, this is my wife Ellen, and it seem you have met my daughter Sylvia." Said Montgomery.

When Ellen and Sylvia were introduced to the samurai, both Ellen and Sylvia kersey.

Montgomery continued, "we have heard wonderful things about your country. So, we decided to come here to ask permission to live here." Said Montgomery proudly.

The man guan again, then he asks. "How many are with you"

Montgomery smile and said, "just my family here."

The man did not say another word to my father, he just turns to the women that was helping us and said in his language.

"You will teach them our ways"

The woman responded by saying, "Hi."

My father asks, who do I have the honored of addressing."

The man turns back to my father and said, "My name is Daiki Ho, I am Samurai. I will check in on you to make sure you are treated properly. However, it is the emperor that will decide if you can stay here or not. Your ship will wait to see what the emperor will say.

After Mr. Ho left, we got our bags together to leave the docks. The woman that is helping us has introduce herself as Chan our guide, she took us to a place on the edge of the village where we stayed for a time. Until we are in our own home.

Montgomery asks Chan, "Who did I have the pleasure of meeting with this samurai?"

"He is one of two samurai that only take orders from the emperor, his name you already know, he is a very powerful samurai some may say he may become Shogun." Chen said.

We settled in what looks like a Cottage. The next morning, we were escorted to a place where we would be staying.

My father must receive the emperor's permission to live here. Later we found out that Mr. Ho talk on our behave.

We purchased a nice sized home. It was surrounded by a large body of land with a beautiful garden that faces the morning sun.

We had trees that blossom in the spring with a beautiful bloom, I have never seen since.

The trees gave us shade in our house throughout the summer.

The Sun set was wonderful, and to see the Sun rise in the morning from the front of our house is breath taking, and I get to see that every morning. We haired a live-in gardener, a good man quite easy going. A thin man with a friendly smile. He was approximately 5ft. 5in. tall and the way he moves was effortless, his name is Daichi, and he became a good friend. My family liked him from the beginning. At the time I did not know how important he would be to me.

During our time in Japan was wonderful, I love our way of life, as a little girl, every morning I would take a walk through the village, and fine myself in front of the place where the lady gave me candy when I first arrived in the country, and just like it was routine the Samurai met me their every day. Mr. Ho, and I will walk together though the village and talk.

Sandy interrupted, "what did you two talks about?"

Sylvia smiled and looked at Sandy and said, "we did not talk about anything important. He would tell me about his people customs, and the way of the samurai. We walked and talked until we arrived in front of my house. My mother and father would meet us on the porch and exchange pleasant words. Mr. Daichi talked with my parents before he left; he bows fully at the waist. As the years pass, I started to see a bond between Mr. Daichi and Mr. Ho.

I said my goodbye to Mr. Ho, then my mother will take me inside while Mr. ho and Mr. Daichi talk as they were walking away from the house. Mr. Ho did most of the talking. After the conversation ended, Mr. Ho would bow silty and walk away. At the time I did not know that Mr. Ho was preparing me for his future.

Mr. Ho is a great warrior and has roses through the ranks fast. Though some of the other samurai did not show it, they were very jealous.

I did not know that I was a big part of his plans to reach the Shogun, and Mr. Daichi was getting me ready for something big.

Later Mr. Daichi started to teach me Jujitsu, and it was fun. This is when I found out that Mr. Daichi was no simple Gardner, he was a Jiu jitsu master, a ninja. We will practice every day. Daichi taught me everything he knew, and it would take years to learn. One day I had to asked him, "Where did you learn all of this?"

We stopped practicing and sat down across from each other.

Daichi said, "I belong to a clan, I will not tell you the name of the clan because it is forbidden, it would endanger you and your family for me to teach anyone the ways of the ninja outside of the clan. There are only two people knows that I am teaching you this, General Ho, and myself, and you are not to speak of this to anyone that includes General Ho. If anyone finds out they will put you, me, and your parents to death."

He made me promise him not to tell anyone, not anyone, not my parents, not anyone.

Sylvia said, "Why can't I talk to Mr. Ho about this?"

"Why do you want to talk to him about this since he already knows?" Said Daichi.

Sylvia look Daichi in the eyes and said, "I give you my word, I will not speck to anyone about this."

Daichi frowned and ask Sylvia, "What does that mean?"

"I do not know; I heard my father say that. I thank it mean you can trust me." Said Sylvia.

After that I started calling him Master.

Ten years went by, and Sylvia became far better than what Daichi could imagine. Out of all Daichi past students he had, Sylvia was the best he had ever seen including himself.

Like I said before, General Ho is in line for Shogun. A rumor had started, that General Ho may be promoted soon, but no one knew for sure. Most of the samurai did not like it, but because of general Ho accomplishment, he was the best choice for the job of Shogun. We found out that some of the samurai began to plot against his life. This is where I came in.

It was easy to know, who it was that dislike General Ho, but he had to have proof of a plot to end his life.

If he wrongly accuses a samurai, it will bring shame and dishonor to him.

Also, if anyone found out General Ho is friend with a ninja he would be put to death.

For a long time, I wanted to ask Daichi my master, how General Ho and him became friend's.

His replied was, "When Ho was a young samurai, He was walking through my village, he came upon a house on fire. Some of the samurai were standing there watching the villagers trying to put the fire out to keep it from spreading. There was a man trying to go into the house, but the flames kept pushing him back, he yelled.

"My baby is inside!"

His wife was on her knees screaming.

Without thinking Ho grab a blanket that one of the villagers were using to put out the fire, soak it in water wrapped it around himself and went through the flame and inside the burning house, the crowed was astonished to see someone do that. Everyone was tense, the woman stops screaming, and the man who tried to go in the house earlier froze.

What seemed like hours, but it was only a moment went bye when the young samurai Mr. Ho came out.

Everyone stared at the young Ho as he bent over trying to catch his breath.

When Ho regain his composure, he stood upright. He walks over to the woman and unwrapped the blanket, and in his arms, there was a crying baby, the baby was fine simply scared. Everybody all around him bowed low some went to their keens in total respect. Ho gave the baby, to the baby's father, who was standing beside the woman, he said to the man. "Please tell me that it was only one?"

The man shook his head no. Then he bowed and said, there was only one. He gave the baby to his wife who stopped screaming and started to cry tears of joy.

The man turns back to Ho, he drops to his knees and said, "I am forever in your debt. Whatever you ask of me I will make it so." Then he put his head on the ground.

Ho reply, "Just consider yourself grateful that the only thing you lost is a house."

At that moment admiration came from the villagers and a lot from the Samurai.

However, jealousy from a small part of the samurai toward Mr. Ho began.

One of the samurais ask, "Why did you do that?"

Daiki Ho answer, "All life is precious."

This act of bravery causes the emperor to favor Daiki over all his peers.

Later Daiki baby, now a young ninja went on a mission and were killed in a battle against the samurai. Although people mourn his loss, it did not last long because he died a warrior's death.

Mr. Daichi and Daiki Ho became and remains friends. But that is another story.

"Please excuse me, I am getting ahead of myself, and off track. Now back to where I was in my story." Said Sylvia.

Two weeks after Ho save the baby, he was awakened from a very pleasant dream to a noise in the next room, he grabbed his sword and entered the next room. In the middle of the room there stood a ninja, his sword still in his scalp and looking at Daiki Ho.

"Why are you here, did you come to assassinate me? Speak, before I separate your head from your body, WHY ARE YOU HEAR?" Demanded Daiki Ho.

The ninja said, "I came to warn you. There is a plot against your life."

"And why should I believe you?" Said Daiki Ho.

The ninja said, "because I owe you, my life." Said the ninja.

Then he kneeled and took off his wrapping from around his face.

Daiki was shock, he could not believe this man is a ninja. But the shock did not last long, he became incredibly angry because his friend had deceived him, he looked at him and said, "Explain yourself or you will not leave this room alive?" Said Daiki.

"The day you saved my son from the fire was the day I pledge my allegiance and my service to you whether you know it, or like it, or not." said Daichi.

Daiki ask, "have you been watching me since that day?"

"Yes, and you made a lot of enemies that day. Samurai do not usually help the peasants. You are a good man Daiki, A man I am proud to call friend. You are going to do remarkable things for our country." Said Daichi.

"Is this what you came to tell me?" Ask Daiki.

"No, I have news to tell you, a warning," said Daichi.

Daiki lowered his sword and told Daichi. "Sit, and tell me what you know?"

"One of my ninjas whose name is Daisuke, he is one of my students over herd two samurai wishes to do you harm. Their names are Akin and Erie." Said Daichi.

Daichi started to say more, but Daiki interrupted.

"Liar! The two men you speck of are two of my closest friends," yell Daiki.

"The two men I name have hate in their hearts for you, ever since you save my son. They have been attempting to recruit others who also became jealous of you, because the emperor favors you," said Daichi.

General Daiki is a very smart man. To show you how his mine works. When he found out that his friend was a ninja, he knew it would fit in with a plan he was developing.

The woman who was helping my family when we first arrived here. I found out from her later, that it was Daiki that arranged for our house and Daichi our gardener that he introduced to us. With instructions to train me.

Daiki and Daichi put a long-term plan into action that involved me.

We knew that his plan would take a lot of time to develop, Daichi told Daiki, "Just stay alive until we can do what you have in mine my friend."

CHAPTER 6

Ninjas

That is why Daichi told me why my training was a secret even from my parents.

To train me, Daichi had to take me far into the woods to keep everything a secret. My parents believed that it was part of my education, and in a way, it was. Although my mother educated me to read and write.

Daichi educated me in the way of the ninja.

My parents trusted Daichi, he has proven to be a good friend.

I ask Daichi again later in my training, "Why I can't tell my parents?"

Daichi said again. "You are very persistent; I will tell this. You are being trained in the ways of the ninja. If you are found out, Daiki, you, me, and your parents would be put to death. So, it is important that they do not find out."

As a ninja my job were to fine out as much as I can about the plots against my friend Daiki, So I was happy to help.

Daiki enemies would always get together at a place in the village with geisha. There, they plot my friend death. To find out what the plans are, I would often pose as one of the geisha women to learn their secrets.

Daichi informs me, "Daiki's enemies have random meetings though out the week but not on the same day, or the same place. They have food and sake, when they meet, in case anyone questions there were-a-bout. They would reply that it is a social gathering."

Sylvia has connections with the geisha women, they tell me where the next meeting will be. What I would do is pretend to be one of the geisha women who served them. The samurai never pay attention to the servant, they feel that the servants are beneath them. So, it is a good change I will not be recognized.

It was early, enough time for me to put my make up on to look like one of the women who is severing the Samurai.

I took my time in getting ready because I needed to look right for the part. The meeting to my understanding is an important one.

During the meeting I got information about Daiki. Even though the Samurai paid no attention to the servant, the other servant did. One servant particularly, her name is Sato.

Sato was new to the group of women I work with. All the women knew why I was there, and they favor Daiki because of the way he treats the villagers, so they cover for me.

Akin, who pretend to be Daiki friend is the main person behind the plots to kill Daiki, but to do that he will require most of the samurai to go along with him. Sato was seeing Akin romantically, she smiled when Akin couth her eyes.

Akin is a small man about 5ft, 7in, and very mean, he is one of the senior samurais is line for Shogun, and the only person standing in his way is Daiki. And Sato knows that when Akin becomes Shogun her status will reach to the highest level. The only woman higher than her is the wife of the emperor, and even then, she will be walking side by side with her.

In the back room she was throwing her weight around giving orders and talking about what her future was going to be like. That is when she focuses on me.

"Who are you, and why are you here?" Sato demanded.

Sylvia said in a faint voice, "I am here to serve the Masters."

"Stay here," said Sato.

Sato ran in to the samurai meeting, and whisper into Akin ear. One of the servants that was my friend told me that Sato was telling Akin, that one of the women did not belong here. Akin eyes widen, he called one of the lesser rank samurai over and told him to take care of this extra woman in case see is a spy. And make sure you do away with the body.

The samurai said, "Hi." And left with Sato.

Meanwhile my friend told me I should leave because Sato is going to point you out to a samurai, and he is going to kill you.

Akin told the rest of the samurai to leave and said nothing of this meeting.

Akin and the rest of the samurai left together.

Sato and the other samurai went to the back room just in time to see Sylvia leave out the back way.

The Samurai and Sato started to follow but, he stops long enough to give Sato a hard look. Sato knew immediately what that meant, without a word, it meant, stay in your place.

When the samurai knew that his look was understood, he continued to pursue Sylvia.

Akin was nervous, he felt that he may have been discovered, and the plot to discredit Daiki may fail. This means death to him, He knew his man had to catch up with this spy, to find out what she knows, and who sent her, before he kills her. So, he thought.

Sylvia ran though the city knowing where she was going. Sylvia knew the city well, from the walks she had with Daiki. Now she knows why they went on those walks. She knew just where to lead him.

Sylvia kept calm and remembered her training. She ran to a remote part of the city where few people were in the streets, she ran down a dead-end alley on purpose. The samurai believed he has corner her; he pulls out his sword and to his surprised. I pulled out mine. When he saw this, he was shocked, he said one word, "Ninja."

His plan was to disarm Sylvia and find out who sent her.

I had no such plan with this samurai. Me and the samurai battle for several minutes, Sylvia was holding her own against him until he made one mistake, he came down with his sword, I ducked under and step to the left side of him, and sliced his stomach open, there, he died in the alley. I look around to see if anyone has seen them. No one noticed our present, after that I used another skill, I disappeared.

I left the samurai body, so someone could find it and start asking questions to make Daiki enemies nervous.

I went home and told Daichi what happened.

Daichi ask, "has anyone seen you?"

"Yes, her name is Sato, one of the servants at the meeting."

"What about the other servants?" Daichi said.

"The other women warn me that Sato was going to Akin to tell him that there is one to many girls. They help me to get away. Sylvia pleaded. The next day, Daichi told Sylvia later that the women who talk to Akin was reported dead, before she could tell anyone her story.

In the Palace there were a lot of angry samurais who were left in the dark, and a lot of unanswered questions.

Sylvia stopped her story and wanted to explain something to everyone around the campfire.

"Let me tell you this, regardless, if a samurai were good or bad who ever kills a samurai, they would be put to death instantly. You must understand this, now, back to my story.

Sylvia told everyone this to heighten the excitement.

It did not take long for the samurais to find out about the samurai that were killed. All the Emperor Generals are summoned to the palace at once. Once the Generals settled down General Daiki began to speak.

Daiki now knows who his enemies are, he decided to expose them. He started with Tomoko, and Kunio.

The two samurai are 5ft. 11in. tall and very fat, they had trouble getting off the floor. These two men are part of the ones who are plotting against Daiki.

When Daiki turns and smiles at Akin, he now realizes that Daiki knows what they were planning, but how did he find out? The spy must have been at all the meetings that we had, but how did the spy know where and when?

That is a question Akin would take to his grave.

Daiki was in control of the whole situation. The only thing the three samurai can hope for is that this whole thing does not call for their death.

Daiki ask the other samurai, "who else, have seen Akin assisted last?"

The samurai that Akin was about to recruit raised their hands, they had no idea what was going on.

Daichi ask the three men, "What was the meeting for, and what did you talk about.

Akiko is one of the samurai a proud man who is very loyal to the emperor and to Daiki, he spoke for the three. "Akin ask us to meet with him for sickie."

"And did you meet with him?" Daiki asks.

Akiko answered, "yes, we did, but before anything was said, one of the servants came in and whispered something to Akin. After, Akin stood up and told us something urgent has come up that requires his attention. He told us that he will get back to us at another time. He excuses himself and tells one of his aids to go with the servant."

"So, Akin was the last samurai that seen his assistant alive. Was there anything else said?" Ask Daiki.

"No, that was all." Said Akiko.

The four men bow at each other, "Thank you Akiko," said Daiki.

Daiki is still in control of the matter; The Emperor decided to stop the meeting until later tonight for unknown reasons.

Daichi took this time to get rid of some loose end in this matter. Sylvia, and Daichi, must leave the country along with Sylvia's parents. He already knew about the ship at the dock. So, he has a plan to use it to carry everyone out of the country.

Daiki met with his friend Daichi and Sylvia to discuss their next move; this time Sylvia parents was at the meeting. The meeting went on for a long time.

Daichi started the meeting by saying, "I may have a way to get you four out of the country. There is a ship that came in. It is anchored at the emperors' docks. The ship belongs to a good and close friend of the emperor, a man that can be trusted. This will be your only way out.

The ship is from your country, so that is where the captain will take you, but we cannot tell him without destroying the friendship he has with the emperor."

Now confuse Sylvia ask, "how are we going to do that."

Daiki said, "we have a lot of time to figure that out, but none to waste. You have another mission. You and Daichi will go down to the docks and find out how long this ship will be here, and their purpose. Then we will know how much time you have for your departure."

"Wait! You said four, you mean my parents must leave too, and who is this other person? Ask Sylvia.

Daiki look at Daichi and said, "I am sorry my friend, but you will have to go too."

Daichi said nothing, he understood that if he did not go, he would have to die to keep from talking, so he just bows in agreement.

Sylvia did not like the thought of leaving the only Country she grew up in, but she understood why she and her family must go.

To find out what she needed to know, Sylvia dressed as one of the docks workers and went down to the docks to spy on the ship. She notices that some of the dock's workers will board the ship to help unload boxes and baskets so that is what she will do.

Daiki stayed on the docks to see what he could find out about the ship. I went unseen aboard the ship. There I seen the most handsome man I have ever seen. I had to find out more about this man, and his purpose here.

I overheard that this man's name was Scott Martin, and the reason he was here. He was here to see the emperor about bringing back some Samurais to his country to train his man for war.

I almost gave myself away by laughing aloud. I knew then that this man's country was in trouble. The emperor will never let his samurai leave the country.

I told my master Daichi, and my friend Daiki about what I heard aboard the ship.

"Their country is getting ready for war, and they are going to ask the emperor to give them some Samurai to help train their men," said Sylvia.

Daiki said, "the emperor will never agree to this, but there may be a way to help them, and at the same time get all of you out of the country.

Sylvia you are the key, to this hold thing, you are going to help these men."

Sylvia's Mother let out a long sigh, she asks her husband, "Montgomery, where are we going to fine the peace that we enjoyed here?"

"We are not going to worry about that right now. First things first, we must get ready to leave," said Montgomery.

Then Montgomery turns to Sylvia and said, "I want you to understand something. Not only will you be helping their country, but you will also be helping yours. That is where you were born."

Daiki said, "I have sent some Samurai to the ship to escort the two men to where they will be staying, until the emperor sends for them, followed them."

Sylvia followed the Samurai to a cottage undetected. And Daiki left to meet with the emperor and the rest of the General's.

At the same time Captain Moore and Scott are taken to the cottage. The Emperor General's was in a meeting with the emperor.

Daiki was angry when he addressed the council. "I have question that needs answered, now?" He spoke.

Daiki asks the two Generals Tomoko and Kuniko. "Did you find out anything about the death of Keiko assistant?"

The two men are Keiko closes friend; they were there at the meeting. Kuniko stood about 5ft. 8in. a master bowman. Tomoko 5ft. 9in. is a master in martial arts.

Of the two Samurai, it was Kuniko that responded. "No, we can't find out anything, it stands a mystery to us."

General Daiki grunted and said, "I have also investigated this mystery, and you are right, I also did not find anything, but I did find out something else. I found someone who knew what the meeting was about."

Daiki turned to the Samurais that were guarding the entrance and gestured to open the door and tell the person to enter.

A female came in. Daiki gestured for her to come near him, then he pointed to where he wanted her to stand. She walked to where Daiki pointed and fell to her knees and put her head to the floor.

Daiki ask Tomoko and Kuniko, "Do you know this woman?"

The two samurai look at the woman and said, "NO."

Then Daiki asked General Sachiko and General Sufi the same question they shook their heads No.

Daiki said, "I understand, because we do not concern ourselves with the servants, but this woman served you four in all the meetings you had throughout the city in plotting my death."

That started all the Generals to talk among themselves.

General Sachiko jumps up immediately grab the hilt of his sword and said, "How dare you accuse me of this crime."

General Sachiko and Suga are high ranking Generals just under General Daiki. These are the two men that was jealous of Daichi, because Daiki were promoted over them.

The emperor intervenes and tells General Sachiko to sit down.

General Daiki continue, "This woman is the one of four who served you two and Keiko at the meetings you had. The attempts on my life come from these meetings."

General Sage decided to speak. "You bring one servant here among us to tell these lies, and you expect us to believe her?"

General Daiki smile and said, "No, I did not thank you will believe this one servant."

General Daiki turned to the Samurai guard at the door and this time Daiki just nodded his head. The guard open the door, and in came three more servant girls, two men and an old woman.

General Daiki said, "Hear are the rest of the servants that were there that night you used in the meeting. The same servants you used in every meeting you had. They are willing to testify in front of the emperor knowing if they lie in the emperor presence it will mean their death. They are here to tell their Emperor that the Generals I have name has been at every meeting and their plans to kill me."

As Daiki was saying this, he was looking at Keiko.

The emperor asks the servant's one question, "Is everything the General said is true?"

Everyone responded at the same time, "Hi."

General Keiko was very selfish and mean, he cared only for himself, not the people, and not the emperor just himself. He is also a coward. He came from a very honorable family. That alone is why he has been promoted to General. A lot of samurai did not believe he was ready to take on the roll as General, and he was not. Keiko is very weak and quite easy to manipulate. Knowing his history, he broke down and admitted everything, and I mean everything.

Keiko asks Daiki for forgiveness, "I am sorry for this awful matter."

Keiko turns toward the emperor, and said, "Please forgive me?"

The emperor dismisses all the witnesses. After the door closed behind them the emperor stood up and did not try to hide his anger. He addresses the three Generals. "Come before me and knee. Because of the dishonor you have shown your Shogun, and the dishonor you have brought before me. Your sentence will be death, I will aloud you an honorable death to take your own life. I will give you this honor that is more than what you give your Shogun."

Three of the four General stood up and disrobe, they keel down in front of the emperor and took out their short sword and push it in their stomach then slice across their belly.

Keiko could not summon the courage to take his own life. Before he could make another plea, his head fell on the floor.

General Daiki stood behind Keiko with his sword out. Blood dripping from it, he had just cut Keiko head off. He checks the other men to make sure that they are dead, then he turns to the emperor and nod.

The emperor told the remaining Generals and said, "We should be retired for the evening, and we will see our guess tomorrow."

At the Martins house, Daichi approach Sylvia in the garden and said, "I have a mission for you."

"What is it you want me to do?" Said Sylvia.

General Daiki is sending four women to the house were the captain, and his General from the ship as a present from the emperor for the night.

"I have made arrangements for you to be one of the women, so you can find out if this General is an honorable man." Said Daiki.

Later that night at the Captain and Scott's house, there was a knock on the door. The captain answers it with a pistol in his hand, he was not expecting anyone. When Captain Moore saw who it was, he said, "come in"

A Samurai came through the door, he bowed and stepped aside. Four women came in with their head down at the floor, the women line up, side by side on the other side of the room.

"This is a gift from the emperor. The emperor will see you tomorrow evening, enjoy yourself." Said the Samurai.

Captain Moore took three of the women with him in the next room. I stayed with General Scott to find out what kind of man he is, what is his purpose heard, and for personal reason.

The captain's friend and I talked for a long time. I learned his name, Scott Martin, and why he is here.

I did not know why this man Scott fascinated me so much, I could have talk with him all night but, I was on a mission.

After I found out what I needed to know, it was time for me to leave. But I could not just get up and walk out. So, what I did was, kiss him on his cheek, and walk to his room at the same time I took off my clothes look over my shoulder at him and said, "I will keep your bed warm until you come to bed."

I disappeared into his room and claimed in his bed.

I did not have time to pull the sheets over me when Scott came into the room, he took off his clothes and jumped into the bed with me. Scott put his arms around me, and we smiled at each other as we moved closer together. I touched his face as our lips got closer. Then I apply pressure to the side of his neck, and he passes out.

While he was unconscious, I went to the door and let another woman in, who took my place in bed.

I left the room thanking that Martin was a good man that love his country.

I could not understand this feeling I have that he is someone that I wanted to be with.

After Martin was turned down by the emperor. Daiki sent a message to Scott at a place to meet Daichi.

When Scott arrived, Daiki was looking forward to the conversation that this General from another land has to say.

The two men talk for a long time.

Daiki told Scott how sorry he was, that he would not get what he wanted and then he gave Scott automotive.

Daiki told Scott there is a way he can have everything that you came here for. That is all Daiki said about that, to keep rumor silent. Instead, Daiki gave Scott a scroll to give to me, to give to my Master. After I left Scott, I went to my Master to deliver the scroll. Daichi read the stroll and told me what it said.

"Daiki has developed a plan on how to get us out of the country. Get ready my child we should prepare to leave tomorrow."

Later that night My Master met with Scott and introduced me as the person he needed to take back, all will be explained later, and a long with her, goose the family and friend.

Daichi and I produced a plan. What I must do is to disguise myself as a very annoying old woman with an attitude and lots of luggage, which includes three large chests. Inside each of the chests will be my father, mother, and Daichi.

When Scott met with my master. I had to throw him across the room a few times, to convince him I can do everything for what he came here. After he was convinced. We put our plan into action.

Daiki told Daichi, "get ready my friend's things are too close to us, everyone must leave tomorrow."

The Samurai do not like annoying women who talk back, and since I am from another country, they were so happy to see me leaving they even help me with my luggage aboard the ship.

The Samurai had an idea what was in the three chests they brought aboard, but they kept quiet.

The ship is where my parents met Scott for the first time, my father liked him instantly. My mother said, "he has a very sincere look."

At the campfire Michelle asked. "Did anything happen on the way back from Japan?"

CHAPTER 7

The Voyage Home

Scott answer, "Well you know it was a long voyage and Sylvia and I grew closer together and fell head over heels in love, during the voyage home she started to train me aboard ship."

"Later I found out that he had a head start in his training, because of the training he received from the Black foot tribe." I was amazed at how fast Martin caught on.

We reach the islands; Martin told me about where he stops at on the way to Japan. That is where we got married." Said Sylvia.

We did not know how long the voyage would take, because after we left the island, we stopped on the west coast. We were considering going across inland but dismissed it. It was faster to go by ship and safer than to go across country.

During our time on the west coast, we stopped for supplies. While the ship was loading our cargo, my mother and I decided to go shopping. Master Daichi asked if he could come along?

As we walked through town, we came to a district that people name Chinatown. This is where Master Daichi wanted to stay.

I said my goodbyes to my Master, I did not know if I would see him again. We left the west coast and went around the Southern continent bound for Washington.

As soon as we entered the Atlantic Ocean, we were boarded by two ships from England they believed we were hostile or spies. Our Captain told them that we were on a voyage back home from Japan. The English man believed our story because of the direction we came from.

The British could not find anything to support their claim of us benign a spy. So, they let us go.

It is funny that the British has no way in knowing that the very people they stop will be the people that will help win the war against them.

We also ran into a ship coming from France, where they were going, I do not know.

The French told us that war was about to start, and we should get to shore. They inform us that the East Coast is overrun with British soldiers.

The French are a very romantic people. The uniforms are very colorful, and their Captain was nice. Although I could not understand a word he said. Captain Moore spoke his language and translated for us.

"To avoid trouble, go further north," translated Captain Moore.

And that is how we came to Canada. In Canada we purchase two Wagons.

Our plans were to drop my parents off at the camp, and then take two horses, and ride toward the East to meet with General Washington.

We pulled into a small town to rest from our trip and to prepare for the journey to Camp in a few days.

The next day Scott, Sylvia, and her parents were having breakfast. Near the end of the meal.

Scott said. "I am going to check on some supplies we would need for our journey, would anyone like to come?"

Mr. Montgomery said, "Yes, I don't mind at all."

"No, I think I will look around town to see what the stores have to offer. Would you like to come Mother?" Said Sylvia.

"No dear, I will just stay in my room and rest. I will see all of you when you get back." Said Ellen.

Scott and Montgomery kissed their wife and went to gather supplies for their journey.

Sylvia asks her mother, "Mother, are you alright?"

Ellen said, "Oh yes dear just tired from the trip."

"Okay, I want be long." said Sylvia.

Then she kissed her mother and left.

Sylvia was walking down the street looking at all the shops, she stopped in a few shops to pick something up for her or her mother and continued walking greeting people as they passed.

CHAPTER 8

Mark

Sylvia started to cross an alley and heard a man talking with an accent she never heard before, but it is not how he was talking, it is what he was saying.

Sylvia heard him say, "Gentlemen please, you have the wrong person. My name is Mark Antony I am from a country called Italy. I am not this person you are seeking."

One of the three man said, "yell, yell, which is what they all say. To me you are just another nigger slave."

The man who was speaking was an impeccably dress man, not a fancy man, but a man with money. The other two men was dirty, always smiling, their wear stained with tobacco, and eager to apprehend this, Mark Antony.

The two men was a step or two behind the men who was speaking. You can tell the two men work for the impeccably dress man.

One of the men was medium build long duty hire, with an oval shape head, he stands about 5ft. 8in. and seem very nerves. The other person is tall, 6ft. 6in. more, or less. He is very muscular with a round shape bald head with one thing on his mind, doing harm to this, Mark Anthony.

Sylvia was going to join the conversation and was ready to fight those three people, but Mark said something that made her hold back.

"Please, I don't want to hurt any of you." Said Mark.

The three men laughed.

Mark said, "But, you don't understand I am telling you this for your own good."

The three men look at each other and begin to laugh aloud. When the laughter clam down the leader said.

"Right, put the chains on him."

The two men step toward Mark. When they got in arm reach. Mark step to the left side of the muscular man, grab his hand and flip him over his back. Then Mark done something that empress Sylvia. Mark took his bow and shot an arrow into the muscular man chest while the man lay on his back. Moving so fast that it was hard to keep up, he took another arrow and shot the oval headed man in the right eye, it came out the back of his head. Before the body hit the ground, Mark had a third arrow out and pointed at the third man. The man put bout hands up in the air and said, "Wait! Wait! Do not Shoot you know you may be right. I think we do have the wrong man."

Mark smile back at the man and said, "too late." And shot him in the head.

Sandy interrupted. "Stop! Okay this is where you and Scott met Mark, right."

"Yes." Said Sylvia.

Sandy taking on the role of director.

"Before you go any further, Mark, please, tell your story. Start from where Sylvia left off." Said Sandy.

Yalonda said, "I would love to hear about your pass."

Mark said, "instead of picking up were Sylvia left off, I will start my story in my country, Italy, our farm was a mile outside of a village called Liguria Vernessa, but just to be clear, my life began when I met Yalonda, since I met Yalonda, I do not think about my pass much, because my thoughts have been on her."

"As it should be." Smile Yalonda.

Everyone laughed aloud.

"But knowing all about Mark Anthony's pass should be exciting, so sweetheart I'll shut up and sit back and let you talk," said Yalonda.

Mark's Story

MARK'S TABLE OF CONTENTS

CHAPTER 1

Mark's Story

Mark smiled at what Yalonda said, then he cut off a piece of meat, put it in his mouth and started to chew. Everyone knew Mark was getting his thoughts together. Afterwards Mark leaned forward and said, "I came from a dishonorable family. My stepfather's name is Angelo, he is a brutal man, he makes his living by robbing people. He stands a foot taller than me with curly black hair. After my mother married him, he became mean and nasty. Of course, his occupation was not revealed until after the wedding. Oh yes! in addition the man became fat.

My real father died when I was an infant. When I was eight years old, my mother whose name is Sienna stood 5ft. 8in. with long black hair, she met and married Angelo. Angelo has two sons Antonio and Piero. Antonio was the oldest he was not very smart, stands 5ft. 11in. long black hair that came down to his shoulders, he is skinny with two front teeth missing and very uneducated, and he is the smartest one of the two. Piero is the youngest, unlike his brother he is short and fat with short hair and very dirty all the time. Piero has been spoiled from birth and he feels whatever wrong he does his father will get him out of it. But they have one thing in common, they fear their father.

Angelo two sons work in the family business of staling food, they enjoy it. My mother tried her best to protect me as much as she could, and for her reward Angelo beat her.

One day Angelo came to me against, my mother wishes, and told me, "Go with your brothers into the village and bring back some food for your good for nothing mother, so she can fix us dinner."

My mother said, "no, stay where you are."

She turns to Angelo and says, "you have Antonio and Piero to do your evil. I will not let you turn Vito into a bad person like you three," At the campfire Michelle said, "who is Vito were did he come from?"

Mark replied, "Vito is my real name, you will understand later. I will continue."

Angelo said, "who do you thank you are, to tell me what I can or cannot do in this house." Then he slaps her hard.

But my mother is not the one that gave up. She fought back hitting and scratching him in his face. Antonio and Piero believe this was funny they began to laugh aloud.

Angelo held her at arm's length then hit her with his fists. That is when I jump between them and said, "Stop, I'll go, just don't hit my mother again."

He grabbed hold of both of my arms near the shoulder and pick me up off the floor and said, "Now you are telling me what to do."

Then he threw me across the room, I landed at the feet of Antonio, and Piero who began to kick me.

Angelo Yelled, "Enough, take him and get some food."

Antonio and Piero picked me up and pushed me to the door, I glanced at my mother to make sure she was all right. She was lying on the floor crying, just before I was pushed out of the house.

We walk to the village plotting what we are going to do. The plan we produced was, I will distract the merchant while Antonio and Piero took what they needed. After the two brothers gathered enough food, they ran home.

CHAPTER 2

Savarino

I stayed in the village; it was the first time I had been away from my house. Everything was fascinating to me. The village had a festival, there were jugglers, men walking on stilts, Magician, puppet shows for children. There were people in a circle surrounding two men fighting, and everyone was betting on who will win. There were a lot more, men throwing knives at a target, and women dancing on stage. But what fascinated me most were this man with a long bow and arrows, he was doing trick shots. I could not take my eyes off his performance.

The man is fit, a slim man with long black hair, and clean shaven, the things he could do with that bow was unbelievable. He saw me doing his demonstration and smiled. After the show, the bowman noticed I was still there. He walked over to me and bent over.

He asks me, "did you like what you seen?" Said the man.

"Yes," said Vito.

Then the bowman asks, "how much did you like it?" He held out his hand.

Vito told him, "I have no money."

He stood up and looked at me, what seemed like the first time, and that is when I met my first nice person.

He said, "it has been a very good day, come let's get something to eat."

We went to a nearby tavern in the middle of the village. He said that I can order anything I wanted. I did not know what to order, so, the bowman ordered it for me. He was talking about the places he has been and the things he has seen. When the waiter came with our food it was wonderful. I never tasted food prepared by someone else other than my mother. We had small talk, doing this time I reviled the truth about why I was here in the village.

The Bowman looked at me across the table and said, "Where are my manners I have not introduce myself to you, my name is Savarino the Archer. I can tell by looking at you my young friend you would like to learn how to use a bow, so, you will not go hungry again?" Of course, I said, "yes."

Savarino said, "I will make you my apprentice, we are going to make a lot of money together. Meet me back here before the Sun come up."

Before I left, I thanked Savarino for the meal. For the first time in my life, I was happy. But that will end when I get home. As I approached our house Angelo met me at the door.

"Where have you been?" Said Angelo.

"In the village." I answered.

He slaps me with the back of his hand and said, "don't get smart with me, you know what I mean."

"It was a festival in the village I wanted to see it." Vito said.

Angelo grabs me by the arm and said, When I send you to the village with Antonio and Piero you come back with them, do you understand me, and since you did not return home with them you will sleep in the shed tonight without supper."

I just walked away toward the shed thinking to myself, "without supper, I smiled, right, too late for that. I have already eaten and eaten well."

The shed was huge, it was like a large room filled with tools that my father used. My real father was a carpenter and a hunter. My mother told me that the tools have not been touched since he passed away.

I was making myself comfortable when the door opened, it was my mother, she sneaked a sandwich under some blankets.

My mother asks, "are you alright?"

Vito smile at her and said, "yes I am."

Vito told his mother to eat the food because he had already eaten. She looked at Vito extremely hard, but did not say a word, she did not have to, her face said it to her. Vito laughed and told her what happened in the village. She warned me not to go back, but I told her. "I must, I could feed us every day. No more stealing for food."

CHAPTER 3

The Teaching

I went on to tell my mother about the man called Severino I met in the village. "Mom he is a good man, and he went to teach me to be good at this archery."

My mother said, "Okay, just don't let Angelo know, no telling what he will do, just be careful please?"

Vito smiles and said, "I will mom."

The next day, I sneaked away from the house and met with Severino. He began to teach me everything he knows. Well months went by, and Angelo had no idea what I was doing. He just believed I ran into the woods to be alone. If I keep bringing home dinner, he will not say a thing.

One day I was doing a show which I am a part of now. We discovered something. Doing the show, we were shooting at a target when Severino hit the target right in the middle. He turns to me and says, "Now let's see if you remember what I taught you had any effect, now top that,"

I smile, look at the target and said, "I can't top that but." I pick up an arrow saying at the same time. "But I can."

I pull back my bow and let the arrow fly, the arrow split Severino arrow in two and stuck in the target. I look at Severino and said, "match it."

I was looking at Severino smiling. He was amazed at the shot. With excitement he said, "I have never seen that before, you have gone beyond my teaching. The student becomes the teacher."

Severino grabbed my arm and pulled me to him, before I could react, he hugged me. Then he said something that shocked me. "I couldn't be prouder of you if you were my own son." Said Severino.

That is when I felt real love from Severino. I felt myself wishing he were my father.

Severino kneel in front of me and said, "one day you will be famous bigger than I could ever be."

But the moment did not last long. I looked to my right and saw Antonio and Piero. When we locked eyes, their smile was very evil. I already told Severino about my family. I also told him what I had just seen.

"I have to go," said Vito.

I started to leave, Severino stop me and said, "I have an idea, come we must hurry."

Later that evening when I came home. Angelo was waiting for me with a rod that he used to beat Antonio and Piero when they did not do what he says. He approached me and then stopped because of what I was holding. I had five ribbits in my hand.

Pointing at the rabbits, he asks me, "What is that for?"

Vito answer, "dinner."

This is the first time I saw Angelo smile.

Angelo told his two boys, "take the rabbits outside, gut and skin them. After, wash them and hand the rabbits over to her. He pointed at my mother, to prepare a feast.

Antonio asks, "Aren't you going to beat him?" Angelo faced Antonio then hit him in the stomach.

"Vito brought home dinner. What did you bring? Nothing! Now do what I said and be quick about it."

Anglo look at Piero and said, "What are you waiting for!" He swung at Piero. Piero duck and ran out after Antonio.

Angelo turned to me and said, "Come in and sit with me. Please tell me more about this man in town."

Vito told Angelo, "He is a good and a respected man that taught me how to use a bow."

Angelo said, "tomorrow I would like to meet this man, do you thank you can arrange that?"

"Why do you wish to meet with him?" said Vito.

"I just want to meet the man who gave such a gift to my boy." Said Angelo.

"I will make the arrangement." Said Vito.

Nothing else was said that night. Vito could not help wondering if Angelo was up to something.

My mother told me later that it was a good thing what I did.

For the first time in a long time its peace in the house.

However, the peace will not last long, from that day on Antonio and Piero looked at me with hate in their eyes, because of the food, I had Angelo favor.

My mother warned me to be careful she said, "I don't trust those two."

The next day I told Angelo I would meet him in town, there was something I must do, and left before he could say anything.

I had to go to town to tell Savarino that Angelo wanted to meet with him. Savarino agrees to the meeting.

Later, I introduce Angelo to Savarino. After I was told to leave. So, the two men can talk in private.

After their conversation, Savarino approach me and said, "get things ready for the day."

Savarino did not tell me what he said, but he seemed concerned. I left it alone because I felt he would tell me later.

Every morning I will leave and run to the village to be with Savarino and later we will go hunting and, than I will go home with my kill.

One day Savarino had something else to do, so, I went hunting, along after I will go home carrying what I kill that day. Let me tell you that I feel comfortable hunting by myself.

One day when I came home after hunting, I went to the shed to hang up my ribbits. After, I went to the house. I saw my mother on her knees facing the door crying. Angelo and his sons were sitting at the table.

CHAPTER 4

The Ambush

When I walk into the room my mother cried out and said, "Vito, don't do it."

Angelo slaps my mother with the back of his hand. Then he turned to me and said, "Sit down we need to talk."

Not knowing what was going on, I sat down. Angelo said something that shocked me.

Angelo said, "I will have a word with you. There are merchants coming to the feasible with a lot of money, we are going to take it from them."

I ask Angelo, "where did you hear this?"

"It was Piero, he overheard talk among the merchant that someone is coming through the forest at noon tomorrow to the festival with lots of money to spend and trade. We are going to take his money and goods and sell it in town, no one will know where we got the merchandise. Here this is how we are going to do it, said Angelo."

I look at him strange and said, "What do you mean we?" Said Vito.

Angelo looked up from the table and said, "we, meaning all of us, you, Antonio, Piero, and me.

Vito stood up, took one step back and said, "I don't want anything to do with this."

Angelo came around the table, he hit me in the stomach and said, "You will do as I say, or I will beat you until you can't walk for days."

I straggle to get to my feet, when I did stand up after Angele punch me, I look him in his eyes and said, "I don't care what you do to me, I won't do it."

Angelo step toward me, then he started to smile, he put his hands on my shoulders and started to chuckle, he taps me on the side of my face with his open hand, Angelo chuckled again and walk away wagging his finger at me. At the same time, he walks toward my mother and said, "Oh yes, you will help us, Angelo reaches down and grabs my mother by her hair, then he looks at me, and said, "If you want to see your mother again you will do what I say. Antonio will stay here with your mother until this is over." Said Angelo.

I was very frightened for my mother, so I said, "What is it you want me to do?"

Angelo looks at me and laughs. "Now that is my boy, all we needed was a little understanding. We will wait in the forest when the merchant comes. Vito, you will shoot and kill the driver and the guards, we will handle anyone inside. Now for us to get away with this, everyone must die. After a week or two we will move to another city, where we will live like kings," said Angelo.

Vito asks, "where are you planning this ambush?"

Angelo replied, "where the road comes closest to the house."

"If that is so, we will be the first to be interrogated about the robbery. It should take place further up the road where the forest is dense. I know this place because I go hunting there, also I think I should leave early to go to the village, to confirm what Piero heard. People in the village like me, so they will open and talk about anything," said Vito.

Piero got angry and said, "are you saying I don't know what I am talking about, are you calling me a liar, I know what I heard?"

Vito said calmly, "No, just to make sure you have not miss anything like how many guards will be with the carriage and what time it is due hear."

Piero did not say another word, he just sat down.

"I will be at the ambush and on time." Said Vito.

Angelo said, "Okay, you will be there waiting for you, or you will not see your mother again. The merchant is coming late in the evening. Vito, make sure everyone sees you so no one will suspect you. Now everyone gets some sleep, tomorrow at this time we will be rich." Antonio and Piero like the sound of being rich.

Vito ran to his mother and whispered in her ear while picking her up off the floor and walking her to her room.

"Don't worry mom I have a plan, after we leave get yourself ready to leave for good." Said Vito.

My mother asks, "where are we going?"

"I do not know yet, but I will after I talk to Savarino, I will let him know what is about to happen. We will produce something I promises, you can trust him." Said Vito.

I went to bed trying to produce a plan on how to get out of this and keep my mother safe.

The next day I left the house early to go into town, still, I have not thought of anything. I met Savarino, as I always do, and as always, he knew something was wrong.

"Okay, before we get started, you like to tell me what is on your mine?" Said Savarino.

Vito hesitated at first, then he took a deep breath, and told Savarino everything. Afterward I felt a large knot in my stomach was untie.

Savarino response was unexpected he begin to laugh.

"You will not believe how many times people try to recruit me for something like that. However, we do have a problem, hmm," said Savarino.

Savarino sat down on his stood and became quiet.

He seems to snap out of his trance, and say, hear is what we are going to do," said Savarino.

Later that evening I went home to join Angelo and his sons with a plan.

When Vito entered his home, Angelo grabbed his arm and said, "Did you say anything to anyone, because if you did, I would kill your mother in front of you, then I will kill you." Vito said, "NO, I spoke to no one.

Angelo said, "what about this person you work for?"

"No one," said Vito.

Angelo just stared at me. He must believe me because he said nothing else. Then he laid out his plan.

"Antonio is to stay with Vito's mother, if we are not back by morning you know what to do." Said Angelo.

Antonio just nods his head.

Angelo said, "okay let's go and get rich."

Angelo, Piero, and I left the house and headed toward the woods, I was feeling better about the outcome of this whole thing.

We entered the woods where the carriage would be bought. Angelo set us up for the ambush, he put me in a tree, and Piero on one side of the road, and Angelo on the other, and then we waited.

We did not have to wait long a carriage was coming slowly around the bend with two escorts.

Angelo yelled just loud enough for Piero, and I to hear.

"Okay, this is it, you know what to do.

As the carriage got closer, I drew back my bow, took carful aim, and one at a time I shot three arrows and three arrows hit their mark, and three men hit the ground.

Upon seeing that Angelo and Piero jump out of hiding and ran to the carriage. When they got close, the three escort that had arrows in them jump up and pointed their pistol at them, then two more men came out of the carriage. One of the men was the constable from the village.

The constable looked at me and said, "Well done Vito and thank you. Now go and check on your mother, we will take it from here."

Angelo screamed from the bottom of his lungs, "Traitor! You will never make it home in time to save your mother, she is dead." Then he begins to laugh.

Back at Vito's house, things were well in hand.

Antonio was getting nervous. His father and brother should be here by now.

Sienna told Antonio, "Now you know your father and brother better than me."

Antonio said, "SOOO, what are you trying to say?"

"Well, when they get the money, they will kill Vito and kept the money for themselves. Splitting the money two ways is better than three." Antonio said, "THREE! My father will never abandon me." Sienna said, "Thank about it, you are the weakest one among the three, even if you could kill me, you are the one that will be apprehended, and trial for murder. Even if you tell the whole story, Angelo and your brother be long gone."

Antonio got very scared, he looked at Sienna and said, "Well, if I kill you now, I can catch up with them. We were going to kill you and Vito anyway."

Antonio raised his pistol and froze, he fell to his knees, and then fell forward. He had two arrows on his back.

Sienna looks up from Antonio and notice a man at the doorway with a bow.

Sienna said, "you must be Savarino, Vito's friend?"

"The one and only, at your service." Savarino replied.

Sienna said, "you came just in time."

"Did not Vito tell you; I like to make an entrance. Now you know my name so, what is yours?" Said Savarino.

"Sienna, my name is Sienna. I am Vito's mother." Said Sienna.

"Glad to meet you Sienna, Vito did not tell me that his mother is so lovely." Said Savarino.

Sienna looks at Antonio corps, and then she looks up at Savarino smiling and said, "I am very happy to meet you Savarino."

Savarino said, "come we must leave this place. We will meet up with Vito in the Village.

When Vito rejoin Savarino and his mother, we made plans to leave, and move to France.

We stayed long enough in the village for Angelo and Piero trail.

During Angelo trail, he stood up and said, "you killed my son. When I get out of here, and yes, I will get out, I am going to hunt you all down, and kill all of you." Then Angelo started to laugh.

After the trial was over, Sienna, Savarino, and Vito decided to move. Savarino was happy to take on the job as our protector.

We decided to move to France. During our journey to France, Savarino taught me how to use a knife and a sword.

We live in France for five years, after, we boarded a ship and went west to Canada.

The trip to Canada was long and boring. I did a lot of practicing on board the ship, which was challenging. The movement of the ship made it a challenge to hit my targets. Sienna and Savarino fell in love and got married on the ship.

CHAPTER 5

The Mistake

I learn English in Canada and other languages as well. We travelled from town to town, putting on our usual show, it was successful, and we made a whole lot of money until Sienna decided that she wanted to settle down.

Savarino said. "We have been doing a lot of traveling, it would be nice to have a place to call our own."

We came to a town that was large, and very populated. This looks like a place that we can live. We decided to stay and get a place to stay, we were planning to settle here until I met Silvia. That day I decided to go for a walk and have a closer look at the city. That is when I ran into some men that had mistaken me for a slave they were pursuing.

The men were slave hunters. The hunters believed that I was someone else. A runaway.

I tried to tell them that they have the wrong man. Then I tried to walk away. One of the men grab me by the arm and spun me around and hit me in the stomach. I was more surprised than hurt. He was more surprised that he did not knock me down.

I responded by kicking the nearest man in the stomach. I try to walk away again, this time two of the men raised their pistol, which is when someone called out. "Look out?" It was Sylvia.

I turn drew my bow and kill the first man. The other man was shocked to see a Black man with a bow and arrow move so fast, Before the man came out of his shock. Vito drew another arrow and kill the second man. I had another arrow out and pointed at the leader of the group. The leader of the group said, "Maybe we did have the wrong man."

Vito said, "too late," and kill him by putting an arrow in his left eye. After I killed the last man, I look at the person who gave the warning. I saw a beautiful woman.

Vito said, "thank you for your warning."

I decided at that moment to start to use my middle name. I introduce myself as Mark Antony.

I started using Mark because of what Angelo said about hunting us down.

The women introduce herself as Sylvia Martin, she said. "You fight with great skill, and courage. There is a place that my husband and I can take you where this will never happen again. Please come and meet him."

When I met Scott, he reviles, a lot of confidence in himself he reminded me of Savarino. Scott told me why he is here.

Scott said, "We are in Canada on a mission. From what my wife tells me you are the kind of person that we are looking for to join us, you see I have an idea of a small group of special people to make a difference in this lawless land."

I introduce myself "My name is Mark Anthony, I travel with my mother and her husband, tell me, if I choose to come with you what is to become of them? Sylvia did not tell me your name." Said Mark.

"My name is Scott Martin, I am pleased to meet you Mark Anthony, and as far as your mother and your father are concern you are all welcome to stay at my camp."

I did not tell him that Savarino was not my father because I like the sound of that.

I accept Scotts offer and shook his hand, and I bow to Sylvia. I felt good when I left the Martins and could not wait to tell my mother and Savarino what happened. Later we all agree to go with the Martin's to their camp.

"This sounds like the place we been looking for," said Savarino.

Sienna agreed. In the next two days, we got ready for the journey to the camp.

We have been traveling for four days. When we inter the new country, we notice six men running after a huge Black man. The Black man was on foot and the six men was on horseback. The Black man stops to face his pursuers. It looked like he was going to put up a fight. We decided to take a closer look at what is going on, but not reveal ourselves just yet.

What I saw surprised me to the highest. This man took on six men at once, and was doing very well at it, until one of the men got behind him and hit him on the head. The Black man went down to his knees. It took four man to hold him down.

One of the men had a big hammer. He must have been the leader because he spoke for everyone, we could not make out what he said, but when he raised his hummer to kill the black man that is when we decided to act.

Sylvia thought of a star in his eye that penetrated his brain. Mark shot the other man in the neck with an arrow. When the other man stood up to see what is happening. The men assumed that the big Black man would stay on the ground, but he did not, the big man got up, pick up the hammer and killed the other four.

"And that is when I met Paul," said Mark.

Michelle jumped to her feet and said, "Waite! Whatever happened to Savarino and Sienna."

Mark smiled and said," Well, why don't you ask them yourself."

Mark pointed to a couple in the middle of the guttering.

Paul's Story

PAUL'S TABLE OF CONTENTS

CHAPTER 1

Paul's Story

By now there were more people around the campfire to listen to the stories on how The Five started.

Susan asks Paul, "My king, have you always been this magnificent?"

Susan started calling Paul her king ever since Paul rescue her from William Bradford as a salve. She was anxious to hear what Paul has to say, "Please my king tell us your story."

Paul took a big drink of his Ale and leaned back, he paused, and took a deep breath then he began his story.

Paul started out by saying, "I am not going to tell you what happened to my people in the mother land where I was born. It is the same story that you have heard many times before. I will tell you this. When I came to this country, I was a baby still drinking my mother's milk. I was fortune that I was not separated from her. My mother was a beautiful woman 5ft. 7in. with smooth skin, and short hair. Because of the way she looks, she was put in the house to work. People told me that my mother came from royalty. An elderly woman raises me doing the time my mother works in the house. However, my mother could only see me doing the evening.

One day when I went to see my mother I was not allowed in the house. The other salves would not tell me why, or what happen to her. I had to put it together bits and pieces from what I heard the other salves talking among themselves.

The Hate

What I put together was young William wanted my mother. He was caught trying to rap her in one of the bedrooms by his father. His father saw William and what he was trying to do and put a stop to it. He forbids his family and all his white workers not to be involved in any sexual ways with the slaves.

My mother disappeared and was never heard from again. At first, I thought she was dead, but later I heard she had been put on a ship, she pleaded to have her baby with her but for reason unknown, her request was denied. I never seen or heard from her again. If it were not for William, my mother would be with me doing my youth.

William was an overconfident young man trying to please his father after what has happen.

William's father was a tall and heavy man with long sideburns and a bushy mustache. He is a no-nonsense man, who keeps a short leash on young William, it started ever since he caught young William in one of the sheds attempting to rap one of the slaves. William's father beat William and told him how discussing it was for him to be with a slave.

He told him he should be more like his twin brother. That is why I sent him to manage our other plantation. You are not ready yet.

William's father's name is Richard, he told young William every day how disappointed he was in him.

A week later Richard ordered William to go to town to pick up some supplies. In town everyone knew what William Bradford has done, but no one said anything because young Bradford's father is a powerful man that owns most of the town.

To gain respect for his son. Richard arranges a marriage between William and with a young lady from a nearby plantation by the name Carla, she is very educated and well respected among the town's people. Which surprised everyone about the marriage. The marriage was to stop him from raping the slave, but that is enough about William for now. There is not much to say about young William's mother, except that she died after giving birth to William.

The marriage between William and Carla was successful. The raping stop, to the delight of all the slave woman. His bride is a very respected young lady which is why Richard wanted this marriage.

Currently, I was a young boy about ten or eleven years, me and the other children liked to play in the fields while our parents were working nearby. Our elders were trying to keep us from seeing how harsh it is being a salve until we are old enough to manage salve life, they had no success. However, all the children could see that the way we are treated was not right. At night the elders will pass the time by telling us how it was back where we came from. I always wanted to return to the country that they described until I met Scott, now I am happy doing the work with him. But I am getting ahead of myself.

To tell you how harshly we were treated. When the overseer disciplines one of the slaves our parents will put us in one of the huts, so we will not see the punishment, but we saw everything though the holes, and crakes in the walls of the huts.

By the time Richard died. I have grown up to be a young man, I grew big and strong. Because of my size and strength, they put me to work on the docks lifting and carrying things off the ships and putting them on the wagons.

William kept his hands off the slaves (women), but after his father death there were nothing to hold him back, and there was no one to stop him from doing what every he wants. Not even his wife and son.

His wife's name is Carla Marshall a pretty woman with deep red hair that comes down to her shoulders. Her dress and makeup enhance her beauty, she is a slim woman and very sociable. She had heard the rumors about William Bradford, but she ignored them because she thought William was over that. So, she forgave him, she was not aware that William had eyes on Paul's mother.

I am told that my mother kept rejecting William's advances. To punish her, William put me to work in the fields. I was the only child that worked in the fields. That was the last time I seen my mother. Some of the slaves say that she was traded, because of her rejection of William. That was the beginning of my hatred for William Bradford and my hate grew from there.

After Paul's mother came up missing, a friend of my mother took me in and look after me along with the other slave woman.

One of the men that I admire, and he had the respect of all the slave, because of the way he avoided the overseas. His name is Joseph, Joe is what we call him. We all though Joe was crazy. He would do things like run away so far, then sneaked back on the plantation like nothing ever happened. He always said, "I plan my getaways, and what direction I need to take, and a destination. So, when I do run away, I will have a route to take and a place to go, no one will be able to catch me."

It was strange to see him sneak away. Sometimes he will begone for days. Then when I wake up, there he is ready to go into the fields. It was like he had never left. Now understand something, he would only do this once every four or five weeks.

The overseer never caught on to what he was doing. When he came back, he would tell me what, and where he had been, so when the time for me to run away, I would know which path to take. With the time he had left before he made his escape, I made a mental map of his escape plan and route. He helps raise me well. I was too young to go with him, because they would notice that I was gone, before he left, I was old enough to take care of myself.

Joe made sure I did not do anything stupid so I would not pay attention to myself, but that did not work because I could not shake the fact that William Bradford separated me from my mother. My hate grew every day, until one day.

William Bradford came to the fields and saw me for the first time. It shows how much he paid attention to his slaves; he did not know who I was.

I grew bigger and stronger working in the fields, and the looks I gave the overseers made them stay their distance from me.

I stood up and stared at William Bradford with hate. The other slaves tried to tell me not to look at him at all, but I did not listen. He pointed a finger at me, but before he could say something a rider galloped at him and said, "We have a runaway." This made the other salve stand up and look at William.

William turned to the overseers and said, "get these slaves back to work and find out who we have missing and get after him."

The rider's news caused William to forget all about Paul.

William did not like runaways when they brought them back, he an example with them. William would hang them by the wrist and give them fifty lashes to the delight of the overseer.

All the slaves that work in the field knew who it was that ran.

Joe, of course, but what William did not know was that he had been gone for two days.

That was the last time we seen Joe. We would like to think that he got away, and that was confirmed when the slave hunters came back a week later without Joe. William was still angry. No one ever got away when his father William Sr. was alive and now this.

William will have to do something. So, the other slaves will have to think twice about running away.

William Bradford started smiling, he produced an idea; William called for his overseers and asked. "Who did Joe fancy?"

The overseers said, "he fancies an elderly woman that he talks to a lot, she works in the fields."

"Bring her, strip her down to the wrist, tie her up, and make sure all the slaves are there. Do not do anything until I get there," said William.

William did not come out of the house until all the slave has gathered.

Everyone was wondering what was going on.

"Bring the woman," said William.

The overseer brought the old woman forward.

The woman's name is Abby Shaw, everyone calls her Ms. Abby. She was a woman in her sixties that stand about 5ft. 1in., a short lady and heavy, even though she still works in the fields, she plays grandma to all the kids, everyone adores her.

Ms. Abby looks confused, she asks, "Sir what have I done? I have not done anything wrong."

"No Miss Abby you haven't, but since you and Joe are such good friends, I am afraid you'll have to take his punishment," said William.

Then William addresses the slave, he said loudly, "From this moment on, if any of you decide to run, your loved one will suffer for it. Whether we catch you or not. This could be your wife your mother, your father, your children or just a friend of yours."

Then he turns to his overseer and said, "string her up." Order William.

Ms. Abby fault and pleaded not to do this, she falls on her knees bagging for her life.

"Please do not do this," Ms. Abby said.

William did not listen.

She has been stripped down to her waist and hung from a pole with her arms apart and her feet dangling in the air.

Paul could not stand by and see this abusive way Ms. Abby is treated, Paul ran to her side and fought off the men that was tiding her up. Then Paul said to William, "I am the one who is closes to Joe if you must punish someone, punish me instead."

The overseer and the other men look at William to see what he is going to do next.

William looks at Paul and said, "What do we have here?"

William said to his overseers, "Well boys, what do we have heard? We have ourselves genuine crusaders. Well, you heard him, string him up."

They bound my wrist between two large poles. I did not resist; the poles had a pulley on the top of each one. William's men pulled on the rope until my feet was off the ground, then they tide my feet so I would not move around. After I was secure, the overseer steps forward with a wipe.

William shouted, "Stop!"

William went to the overseers and took the wipe from his hand and said, "I'll do this myself." William was very brave and outspoken after he tied me up.

I received ten fifteen lashes. I do not really know. He was angry because I did not yell out, but I did pass out. The last thing I remember before everything went black was William yelling something at me, I could not make it out, I did not care what it was.

When I open my eyes, a woman was their attending to my wounds, she was a thin woman in her fifty's crying over me, I told her, "I will be alright, don't cry for me."

She told me that it was a wonderful thing what I did but after the slaves cut me down. William Bradford told the overseer to string up Ms. Abby. Two slaves ran to try to prevent them from harming her. They were killed.

When the old woman was tied and secure, William gave the wipe to one of the overseers to do the deed.

Ms. Abby did not last long she died soon after the whipping started. William Bradford said aloud, "let this be a lesson to all of you, if you ran, I would take your wife, your mother, father, brother, sister, your loved ones, or I will just pick someone out, string them up and make you watch!!"

He started to laugh, then his overseer joined in with the laughter, he turned and walked away. At that time, I vow to kill William Bradford.

Joe taught me a lot. One of the things he taught me is how to leave William's plantation without getting caught, but the idea of what happens when we do leave, that it will put a loved one in danger. That stopped the runaway since Joe left.

There is something else Joe taught us, to have a plan.

So, I was patient, I bide my time. I knew I could not just walk into William house and kill him. I would not make it to the door. I must have patience; I knew it would take time.

Meanwhile new slave came to the plantation one of the females caught my eye, to me, she was beautiful. She was tall and slender, with short hair. Her name was Ebby. Right away she saw hate in my eyes, at first, she was afraid to even talk to me. The other slaves inform her what happened to Ms. Abby and me. That is when Ebby's heart went out to me, she wanted to get to know me better. I found out where she was from. Although she did not know my people, she did hear a story that the village I came from was often attacked by slave hunters.

CHAPTER 3

The Deception

The time I spent with Ebby, the more I found out how much we have in common, and the more I want to be with her. We spent a lot of time together, For the first time since I was a child, I was happy. We soon got married, and we had a boy. I made up my mind to teach my son that there is a life other than slavery.

It was not long before William started to lust after the slaves again. This started when he found one of his men trying to rape a slave. He did not intervene, he just watched. The next day he gave the man other duties that did not have contact with his slave.

The lust had gotten so great that he produced a plan to have sex with his slave woman. William would see a slave that he wanted and have her work in the house. Once the slave moved in, it was just a matter of waiting for his wife to go into town for one thing or another. Then he would isolate her in part of the house.

William would tell the woman not to yell, and if she did, he would string her up and wipe her daily until you are dead.

There was one woman that refuse. William did the same to her as he does to run-a-ways. He made her watch while William's men wipe her 17year-old son.

After a few days he sold her to another plantation owner but kept her son. William's salve women became very nerves. They feared who was going to be next.

A slave woman produced a plan to stop the rapping of the slave women. She would offer herself to William, so William would be concentrating on her instead.

Her name was Mabel, she stood 5ft. 9in. her hair was short, and her legs were long and slender. She has a petite body, very shapely.

The reason she offered herself to William Bradford was because. This way he will leave the other women alone. However, she knew that she could not just walk to him and say take me and leave the other slave women be. So, she decided to flirt with him very softly, enough for him to notice but not too much to throw herself at him.

Mable makes eye contact with William and smiles then she would walk away slowly looking over her shoulder. William saw this and immediately had her work in the house, and when William wife and child left to go into the town William went looking for her in one of the bedrooms where she was cleaning.

It is a big house and William lost time finding her. William finally came across her in a bedroom in the north wing of the house near his son's room. Mable was alone as she planned, William stood in the doorway just looking at her. Mable knew William was there but did not turn around.

William stepped in and closed the door behind him. Then he gave her the same speech he always gives before he has his way with her.

To his surprise she was agreeable. Mable took her own clothes off.

After, Mable was on the house staff for a long time. Her plan was working, William can have this woman without her fighting him, and she likes what he is doing, so he though.

The rapping of the slave woman stops. The other house slave was able to take care of the house without fear of being attacked by William. They did not know what Mable plane was, all the slave was thanking that Mable likes the attention she was getting from him. Until one day one of the house slave Linsey was her name ask Mable, "Why are you doing this, what do you thank you will gain?"

"Gain from this Mable said? Nothing, I want nothing from William. I am doing this, so our sister does not have to." Answer Mable.

"Oh, good Lord in Heaven." Said Linsey in shock.

Mable smile as she looks at Linsey and said, "how does it feel to do work without fear of William walking behind you?"

With tears in her eyes Linsey gave Mable a hug and said, "you are sacrificing so much. Thank you, I will tell the others so they will be grateful too, for what you are doing.

Mable stops Linsey, and told her, "No, please, if to many people know, William will find out. Let everyone keep their thoughts on me, that will keep me alive.

Mable has suffered hardship from the other house slaves they will not eat or socialize with her. They are avoiding every chance they get. It would be lonely if it were not for Linsey.

This went on for a long time until Mable got pregnant, she was scared to tell William, but she realized she had no choice but to tell him.

When Mable told William that she is with child. William eyes open wide, he sat on the edge of the bed and did not say a word.

Mable did not know what to do next, she was very scared of how William would react. To Mable surprise William did not say a word he just stood up and walk out. For the next two days William tried to produce a plan to handle this pregnancy so his wife would not suspect anything.

He was also worried about the unborn child. What color would it be, what will his wife say or do? William was worried about what his son would think when people found out what he did. He would not have an heir to the plantation, and his wife would leave him.

CHAPTER 4

Revenge

One day when his wife and son went to town, he called Mable in his office, William told her his plan for the baby. "My wife could never know. I will get one of the male slaves to say that the baby is his. I can arrange a marriage between you two. So, my wife will not be wise. If the baby is born Black you and your husband will raise the baby, but if it is white, the baby would have my men to get rid of it." Said William.

Mable did not like the thought of her baby being kill. She did not like this at all. She did not know what to do, she talked to the only person she could, Lindsey.

Lindsey said, "What are you going to do?"

"I don't know, I suppose I have to tell his wife." Mable said.

"What?" Lindsey was surprised at what she said.

"Miss Bradford is the only one I can thank of to protect my baby." Said Mable.

Lindsay asks, "What can I do to help?"

Mable answer by saying, "you have been such a good friend, I do not want you to get involved, I will not mention you. Thank you for being there for me?"

Mable and Lindsay hugged each other with tears in their eyes. Lindsay was concerned about her.

One day when William left to check on his grin mills. Mable went to see if she could speak to William Bradford's wife Carla to tell her what's been going on every time she goes to town. Mable also told Carla about the baby and what William had planned. This would be a mistake she will regret later.

After Mabel had told Carla everything, Carla smile and look at Mable and said, "I was told that William was laying with one of the slaves, but no one knew which one, and if I find out I am going to leave him."

Carla took Mable by the hand and said, "I am glad you came to my child and explained what is going on, you are a very brave young lady. I can see why he picked you; you are a very pretty thing. I told William that if I have proof that he is having any involvement with any of the slave women that it will be over between us. I would leave, and he will never fine me."

Carla thanking to herself," I will come with a plan and after, I will soon put it into action."

Carla then said to Mable, "if you are coming to me for help, I am sorry I cannot help you, you were lying with my husband. But do not worry your head about anything child, I will keep your secrets.

William did not touch Mable after hearing what she told him, or any other slave. He was concerned about Mable unborn child.

Two weeks later William wife, put her plan into action.

Carla told William that she was going to visit her father for a few days. William kisses his wife, and he goes to town thinking that this is his chance to do something about Mable.

Before William could get off the property, Carla put a few things of hers, and her sons, into a traveling bag. After she told one of the men what she is planning to do, he decides to go with her, because being one of William's men on the plantation was the type of work he did not like.

Carla informs the house slaves, "I am going to visit my father for a few days. Tell William I will see him when I get back. She left and was never seen or heard from again.

When William returned home the house slaves met him at the door, when he walked in, they told him what his wife said.

William said, "but she did say she will be back."

One of the house servants said, "yes in a few days she said."

This news made William happy, now he can clear his head and produce something about Mable.

For a week now things were going well, but William still has not produced an answer, about Mable and her unborn child. So, he decided to go with his original plan that was to get rid of the white baby and keep the black one and married Mable off. Another week went by, and William was wondering when his wife would return.

William really does not care if his wife returns or not, it was his son about which he was concerned. After all there are only two people in this world he really cares about, his son and himself. A few more days have pass, William wife still have not returned, he summoned a few of his men to go with him to his father-in-law's plantation to get his wife and son.

The next day William ordered Bruce, one of the slaves, to get a horse and buggy. He left the plantation with a couple of his men for his father-in-law plantation to bring back his son. Paul was told to drive the buggy.

When William got back, he was incredibly angry. Paul found out from William's father-in-law's house slave that his wife had left him, and took his boy with her, and would not return. Where she went was West, where West they do not know.

Paul could not help feeling that it served William right.

William was so embarrassed and hurt that he did not come out of his house for a week. He sent men out to fine them, but they came home not knowing where they went. When William heard this, he became very mean, even more than he normally been. He was cussing everyone for weeks because he could not fine his boy.

William finally came to his senses and picked up where he left off, and that is Mable. He told one of the house slaves to tell Mable to come join him in his study. William told her, "Do not worry, nothing will happen to your baby you can find comfort in that. So, take care of yourself all will be okay.

Doing all this Paul found the right time to practice what Joe taught him on how to run away. While everyone was paying attention to Bradford's problem it was easy to slip away and back.

One day when I made it back to the plantation just in time William returned from town.

Months passed, Mable had her baby, and it turned out to be black. With that news all the slaves knew what William said, if the baby was born Black. This brought relief throughout the plantation. Everyone believed that the baby would not be harmed.

But William plans has change, he decided to get rid of the Black baby, the reasons were he what is an air to his plantation, and a black baby will not do. William did not want a Black person thanking that he owns a part of his Empire. No, that will not do.

Mable was weak doing her recovery. She had no idea what William did. He untied the umbilical cord, and the baby bladed out.

When Mable regains consciousness, she asks for her baby. The house slaves turn and look at Linsey. Linsey was nervous, her face showed great sorrow, you can see Linsey was trying to find words to say, Linsey took a deep breath, then she told Mable what William had done.

To Linsey surprise a strange look came over Mable face, no one ever saw her smile again.

When Mable was able to go back to work, she told no one what she was planning, not even Linsey. Linsey, the only friend she had, knew Maple was up to something, but she did not know what it was.

Without anyone noticing, Mable picks up the linen and a large knife from the kitchen. Next, she went up to the second floor to make the bed in the Master bedroom, Knowing William will be there.

William walks into the bedroom and smiles at Mable he said. "I am happy to see you have gotten better."

Mable turns to face William with hate in her eyes, her head was down with her hands behind her back.

William walks over to her with a big smile on his face. He reaches out to her to give her a big hug.

When William got close enough thanking Mable will hug him back, instead Mable hand came from behind her back with a large knife. The knife is about a foot long, on one side it has a Jagged Edge, and on the other side it is smooth and sharp, and slightly curved at the tip.

Mable raised the knife high and brought it down into William's arm, to his surprise.

"You kill my baby, Now, I will kill you, and I hope you will rot in hell." Mable said.

Mable came at him again with the knife held high, this time he moved out of the way, and knocked the knife out of her hand. Mable recovered and picked up the knife, then she slaps his face and said, "I hate you from the bottom of my heart."

William looks shocked, he told Mable, "Why! I gave you everything that I can give!"

Mable replied, "you did not let my baby live!" She steps forward with her knife held at her waist. William stepped forward and Mable cut him on the arm again, he was still able to grab her arm with the knife. The two wrestles for it, William was able to make Mable let go of the knife, and it fell to the floor.

Without her knife Mable began to scratch and hit William in his face.

After a couple hits, and scratches, Mable put her next plan into action, SHE RAN. She turns and runs down the hall, down the stairs, and out the back door. She left William hurt and badly bleeding from his arm and face.

By the time he had his arm and face attended to. Mable had a head start.

It was late afternoon when William caught up to Mable. He did not realize until now how much he cared for her.

She was untouchable by the white men that work on the plantation, even though the slaves hated her for what she was doing. Whatever she wanted she got, because of fear everyone had for William.

Even though William will not admit he was in love with her. And could not show her how he felt. However, she will never be the same, because of what he did. William could not show favoritism toward Mable, and he told one of his men to put her on her knees.

Mable looks at William knowing if she begs for her life, she will get it, and to do it will sicken her to no end. It would mean that she forgave William for killing her baby.

No, that is unbearable to forgive him, she could never forgive him. Death is the only thing left, and Mable welcome it.

But, before William said anything, Mable stared at him and reached out her hand, and pointed a finger at him. At first William believed this gestor was a plea for mercy, how wrong he was. What Mable said next scared William to the bone. Mable said "You will die at the hands of one of your own salves.

William moves closer to her until his face was inches from her face and said, "I do not believe you; my slave fear me. Just then Mable head butted William and started to laugh.

"Shoot her," William ordered.

What William order brought joy to the overseer, because of the way William treated her, she had the run of the whole house. No white man could touch her, she thought she was better than us white men. Yes, the overseer will take pleasure in shooting her.

The overseer pointed his rifle at Mable's head and pulled the trigger, Mable fell dead at his feet.

William said, "bring her body back to the plantation.

When William and his men got back to his plantation, he had his men to gather all the slave.

All the slaves were assembled in front of William's house, he yelled, "bring her out." His men drag Mable's body out by her hair, at the same time William yelling to all the slaves, NO ONE RUN'S FROM ME!"

William left Mable's body in front of the gathering, turned, and went to his house. The overseer smiled and went wherever overseer go.

Doing the time William went after Mable. Linsey told the other slave why Mable laid with him.

The slave was surprised and became sad. Except for Linsey everybody realizes the sacrifice Mable made. The woman felt very a sham on how they treated her. Linsey let everyone know that Mable did not want everyone to know, because it would give her away.

Mable made a sacrifice for all the women slave until William killed her baby. After that, she seeks revenge, and she was killed for it.

After weeks, his attention was focused on raping his slaves again.

Although William have not gotten around picking out another woman that he wanted. Mable spoiled him to the point he had no desire in laying with another slave.

Meanwhile William received some more slave to the plantation.

There was one slave with a bad attitude, He did not care about anyone at all, the only thing he does care about, is himself.

His name is Jed. Jed is a runner. He let everyone know that he was not going to stay around long.

The slave tries to warn Jade what would happen if he ran. But Jade did not care.

Now Jed is a big man as big as Paul but slow. He did not have a plan at all on how he was going to escape. When night came Jed ran.

The next day William was notified that Jed was gone.

William was about to go into town to get supplies with two slaves from the house and Paul to manage the heavy lifting. Paul has done these many times this was routine for him.

Paul would kiss his wife and hug his son. He got on his knees and told his son to look after his mother while he was in town. His son would smile and say, "okay daddy."

On this day William decided to go after Jed. He had one of his men to take his place to get the supplies. He told another one of his men to get his horse we are going after nigger.

Later that evening William brought Jed back, but the supplied wagon has not been returned yet. The men who took the supplied wagon into town, stop at the Saloon to have a few drinks, this prolongs them coming back to the plantation.

William did not care about the supplied wagon that had not returned, what he did care about was this slave who dared to run away. He caught up with Jed, William's men tide his hands, and was made to walk behind his horse, when Jed could not keep up, he was dragged.

William told his overseer to gather the slave.

"Put Jed on his keens," said William.

William told the slaves, "You know my policy, you run, someone close to you will pay, or I will pick someone at random. So, who here is close to this fool?"

One of William men said, "he is a loner"

"Then pick someone," said William.

The men went through the slave and pick a woman in the middle of the gathering.

The women William men pick was Paul's wife. She did not know what was going on because no one had run from William's plantation since William bought her. She struggles against the men, at the same time calling out for Paul. The only one that responded was her son. He came out to fight against the men to protect his mom just like his daddy told him to do. But he was no match for William's men.

William yelled, "string them both up."

Two of the slaves ran over to stop the men but was shoot.

Both mother and her son were whipped until they passed away.

Jed believed he was next, but when all of William men walk away, he was relieved.

CHAPTER 5

The Plan

When I came back to William's plantation. I found out what happened. I went to see Jed. When I found him, I said, "The first change I get, I am going to kill you."

Jed smile at Paul and whispered, "well you better do it soon, because I am leaving in about two days."

"Not if I am alive," Paul said.

Paul balled his fist and hit Jed hard in the mouth; Jed fell to one knee, but he came up immediately and hit Paul in the stomach.

To the overseers this was fine entertainment they love to see two slave fight, and when you have two slaves as big as these two it brought William's men from other parts of the plantation just to watch. It also brought William out of his house.

Jed was trying to keep Paul off him, and Paul was trying to kill Jed. When Paul started to get the best of Jed. That is the time when William put a stop to the fight. He orders the overseers to break them up. The overseer saw that Paul trying to kill Jed as the overseer and his men pull them apart. After the fight, we were not allowed to work together. Until one day. William had a meeting with all the plantation owners in the area. The fight between Jed and Paul gave William an idea. The meeting took place at William's plantation.

The owners were treated like kings. They talk about things, like new slave coming in, and what part of Africa to get the big slaves. William stood up and got everyone's attention. "The purpose of this meeting was to have a fight every Friday and Saturday among the slaves that represent their plantation. We can put our best slave together to fight and bet on the outcome," said William.

William told one of his men, "go get Paul and Jed."

Jed was working on the docks when he was approached by one of William's men, he said, "Hey nigger Mr. William wants to see you."

Jed said nothing, he just stops working and follow the men to William's house.

William also sent two of his men to get Paul, That, was a different story in getting Paul. The men were talking among themselves.

"Don't get too close to this one he is a mean nigger." Said one of the men.

They approached Paul during the time he was working in the fields. One of the men said, "hey boy, come here."

Paul stood up and stared at this man for a long time. The two-man put their hands on their guns. Paul took a step toward them; the men took a step back. Paul said, "what do you want?"

One of the men nervously said, "Mr. William wants to see you in the house."

As I was walking toward William's house, I could not help but wonder what William wanted from me. I will find out when I get there.

When I entered the house, and stepped into the ballroom where William and some of the plantation owners were, I recognized some of the owners from visits to their plantation, when William needed a slave to do some heavy lifting. Some of the other owners, I did not know.

I saw that each owner had one slave with them. That is when I found out why I was sent for. The owners are going to put the slaves together to fight and take bets on who will win. I could not help to thank about Jed, and how I wanted to put my hands around his neck.

I am ready to leave this life of slavery, but I need to figure out how to do this. I must produce a plan to kill Jed and leave without putting anyone in danger.

Oddly enough, William gave me the answer. Paul and Jed were about in the room hearing what the owners were planning. I produced a plan of my own, I can get revenge, run away without my friends getting hurt.

The plan I produced will be a surprise to everyone. I will become friends with Jed. When I decided to run, the person closes to me would get punished, and since we would be such good friends, he would Jed would be the one to be punished, because William would thank that he has something to do with me running, since he ran-a-way before he plans to run again.

William had the plantation owners and their slaves to step outside. William was the last one to leave the house. Before He join the rest of the plantation owners, he had words with Paul and Jed. "If you two make good on these fights, I will build a two-room house for each of you. If you win, you will not have to work in the fields or the docks. You will only fight once a week, and all you must do is win. Can I count on you?

Both Paul and Jed said at the same time, "Yes sir."

As they followed William outside, Jed told Paul that he was sorry about his wife and son.

Jed had to apologize to Paul, he would not be able to fight and wondering what Paul would do behind his back.

To Jed surprise Paul extended his hand and said, "You didn't know," and left it at that."

Paul knew what William said in the house, what he meant was shack.

When I am ready to run, I will make my move when we are away from the plantation. Now the question will be when and where? It cannot be too soon. I must fight a few fights to get our guards comfortable enough to let their guard down.

Doing all this time one of the slaves came to me and said, "We are all confuse why are you so friendly with Jed."

Paul grin and said, "I am planning to run, and guess who will be wipe for it, my new friend?"

The slave said, "Aaa very smart, but do you thank William will pick Jed?"

"Oh yes! Because he will thank that this is what bout of us plan." Said Paul.

"When are you going to run?" Said the slave.

Paul replied, "I don't know that will depend on the guards."

William plan became popular, other plantation owners from other states heard about what William was doing, and they came with their Champion slave to participate in the fight.

William charged twenty dollars to watch, two hundred dollars to the owners to have a slave to fight.

They came from all over the South, to beat Paul, and Jed, and with them came a lot of people and a lot of money.

Jed and I have beaten all the owner's slave around the area. So, the owners around the area decided to make some real money, by betting on Paul and Jed against the other plantation owners from other states.

With the plantation owners came people from other towns as far as Kentucky, Georgia, Virginia, North Carolina, and a lot of other States like Tennessee, South Carolina, Mississippi, and Texas.

Not only the plantation owner prophet, but the towns people also benefit too. The people that came had to have a place to stay. Hotels are to be built, restaurants, saloons, stables, and other things like shops that will accommodate visitors.

The plantation owners around the area saw an opportunity in making money. They finance the buildings that had were built in town and training areas that the fighter will need before their events.

I hate to say I made William a lot of money. The guards were so comfortable and relaxed having me around going and coming to different fights, there were times I was not chained, when I got in the back of the wagon, instead of coming straight to the plantation, the guards will take a detour into town to celebrate with the money they made.

Sometimes they will meet with women and spend the night.

At first William was a little concerned about this but since I was always with them when we came back, it was okay, Jed would be in another wagon. William did not want us to travel in the same wagon to keep us from plotting an escape.

One evening after a fight there were only two guards to watch over me. The other wagon went straight to the plantation, on our way into town I made my move.

When the road took us through the woods, I attacked the guard that was driving the wagon. Then I grabbed him by the head and broke his neck. After, I took the dead man's gun, and shot the other man that was on horseback. I unhitched the horse from the wagon and turned them loose. I took the wagon and hid it in the forest, I kept their guns and ammunition. I mounted the horse that belong to the man I shot. I remember saying to myself, "I don't thank Joe though about this." Then I rode off.

Back at Williams Plantation. William got all the slave together the next day after Paul ran-a-way.

Jed and the other slave did not know what was going on but, when William get all the slave together, this cannot be good.

William came out of the house and said, "You know my policy when one of you runs someone close to that person will be punished. William asks his men to whom was Paul close?"

His overseer said, "Jed."

When Jed heard his name, suddenly everything made since, why Paul was friendly to him. Paul was planning this all along. Knowing what was about to happen Jed tried to run, but only made it a few yards until he was caught. He begs William, "Please do not sir, Paul, he had this plan all along.

William could not believe a slave was that smart. So, William said, "You are lying, strain him up.

William beat Jed until he was unconscious. Jed disappeared from the Plantation after that, some said he was in chains and put aboard a ship. He has never heard from me since.

I had a large head start, and I bypass towns, Joe told me that is how the slave hunter's track you down by asking people, to have they seen a run-a-way salve. People would be happy to tell were the salves are.

If you go into town people will notice you. When the slave hunters arrive in town those same people will point you out. So, I believed that if I bypass the towns all together. It will be harder for them to track me.

I bypass as many towns as possible that I could. I figure the more towns I bypass the better off I was.

It never occurred to me where I was going, I just no, I needed to get as far away as possible.

During my escape I met some Black people that was not slaves, they gave me some direction, and said, "go north if I wanted to remain free." I thank them and go in the direction they gave me, North.

I live off the land as much as possible, but I knew one day I must go into a town.

After I skipped a few more towns, I would have to go into the next town to get a few supplies like soap, and a change of clothes. I did not have much money, just the money I got off the guards I killed, and I cannot buy anything that will arouse suspicion, a black man with money. unheard of. I had to get further North were nobody cares if a Black man has money or not.

The time came when I had to get some supplies. In the next town I came across, I waited until dark and went into town unseen, to get some things I needed. I pried open a store window and went inside and got everything I needed. I did not know how much money to leave so I left a lot. I made sure I got all the supplies I could carry.

I did my best not to break anything. I slip back out the window from which I came and close it behind me. Then, I made my way out of town. However, I did not realize later I had to get rid of everything.

Joe has always told me to move at night. One night as I was riding along a road that seemed deserted, I came upon a group of run-a-ways slaves, where they were coming from was unimportant, but what they said to me was.

At first the slaves did not want anything to do with me, because I would bring too much attention to them. I had to ask why?

"Why are you avoiding me? I am a run-a-way just like all of you?" Said Paul.

The reason they told me were, "Because you are on horseback, if anyone see you, they will remember that, and which way we are going." Said one of the slaves a female her name Harriet she was smart and knew what she was doing.

What she said made a lot of since to me, so I dismounted, took the bridle, and saddle off the horse and turn him lose. I will finish my journey with my new friends on foot.

We walked all night, and when the sun was about to come up, we needed to find cover, so we could not be seen doing the day.

When we came upon a farmhouse, we used the barn to hide doing the day. The person who owns the farmer only comes into the barn twice a day, in the morning to pick up the tools he needs to work with in his fields, and at night to bring the tools back. We watched the barn until the farmers left. Then we all snuck into the barn and bedded down for the day to get some sleep. I volunteered to stand watch, because I needed time together my thoughts, being alone give me time to plot on how I am going to kill William Bradford. I did not know how, and I did not know when. But I do know I will kill him some day.

When the sun was high in the sky. Bill, one of the run-a-ways, a tall man, he stands 6ft. 10in. slim and kind, an amebiasis man, he has an idea of what he wants to do when he is free. Halfway through the night Bill came to relieve me so I could get some sleep.

Bill was a good man, easy going and very friendly to me, he said, "When the sun starts to go down, I will come to wake up everyone before the farmer comes back. He was always smiling and wanted to be free ever since he was a young boy.

Bill came from a plantation fifty miles North of William Bradford plantation. He decided to leave after his mother passed away. He and the other slave plotted carefully on when to escape. When the time came, the escape was successful because of their planning.

They had no fear of what might happen to the slaves they left behind, because the owner of the plantation punished those who escaped, not the ones they left behind. So, their plan is simple. DON'T GET COULT. I shook Bills hand and found a place to lay down to sleep.

It was late evening when I awakened abruptly. It was a slave hunter four of them. I looked around and the slaves I was with were in chains. The slave hunters caught them trying to run.

Bill was not one of them, he was in the loft when the slave hunters came, the hunters had overlooked him. Bill caught my eye and pressed his finger to his lips to indicate to be quiet.

Three of the hunters came into the barn to see if there were any more slaves. They had one of the slaves with them. His hands were chained.

When the hunters were in the right place, Bill jumped down on him and knocked him down. He put his knee in the hunter chest, while the slave hunter was trying to catch his breath. Bill picks up a large stone and with all the strength he could muster hit the man in the head repeatedly. That is when I made my move. I jumped up and hit the other hunter in the face as hard as I could. He fell backward and landed on his back, I jumped on top of him and kept hitting him. The third slave hunter was about to attack me from behind, but he was stop in his tracks. Will, the slave that was in chin, had the chin around his neck and was choking him.

The fourth man saw all that took place he decided to get on his horse and as fast as he could, got the hell away from there.

One of the hunters who we killed had the keys to the chain. Harriet picks them up and free the salves.

She said, "quickly, gather everything we must leave, now!"

Just then the barn door open and the farmer stepped in. We turned to look at him, we just looked at each other, no one moved.

The farmer looks at the chains, and the three dead man. He knew what had happened. He started to walk toward us. All of us prepare to fight. He looks down at the three men as he steps over one and spat on the other, then he said, "Slave hunters disgusted, the things men do for money."

He then turned his eyes toward us and said, "You let one get away, I saw him run away like the coward they are."

We still have not said a word, but what the farmer said next answered all our questions.

The farmer said, "because you let one get away, he will be back with others, it will not be right away, because the people in these parts feel the same as I do about slave hunters. So, it will be hard for him to get help, you should begone by then. Go down to the smoke house and get some meat for your journey, but hurry the sooner you be on your way, the moor time you could put between you and the slave hunters." The farmer said.

Harriet spoke for us all, "thank you."

"May God see you through your journey, now go," said the farmer.

The woman in our group could not help their self, they hug the farmer before leaving.

The farmer pointed at the three dead men and said, "I'll take care of this."

As the run-a-way left. One of the women look at Paul and said, "I knew it, you led them to us they were tracking you and found all of us." Paul said, "they weren't after me they were after all of you."

"How do you know this." Said the woman.

Paul answers her calmly. "Because if they were coming for me, they would have more men than this. I am considered dangerous from the plantation I came from, and they are right I am extremely dangerous.

Three days have passed since we left the farm. On the third day the runaways and I parted company they turned and went west, and I continued north.

It has been two weeks now since I last saw Bill and the run-a-ways, and just when I started to relax and feel what it is like to be free, all hell broke loose.

It was just after the sun went down when I continued my Journey, I was walking at night in the open, I knew I could not stay in the opening for long, I must find cover, some place before dawn. I do not know what made me turn around, but I did, and what I saw made me start running. I saw six men on horseback headed toward me fast. I felt if I could make it to the woods that was just ahead, I might have a chance to fight them. They easily caught up with me just inside the woods.

I just entered the woods when they surrounded me and dismounted. One of the men I recognize he was the same man that help chain the rana-ways back at the barn were the run-a-ways and I kill his three friends. He looks at me and said, "you didn't thank you would see me again did you boy."

I replied, "no, after I saw that yellow streak down your back when you ran from the farm. I thought that would be the last time I will see you."

Another man who I believed to be the leader said, "you have some mouth on you nigger."

The leader was a big man and ugly too. He loves to bark out orders, and with him he carries a large hammer.

The leader said, "Would you like to know how we caught you boy?"

"No," said Paul.

He ignored me, and went on to say, "Vernon hears (the man that ran from us at the farmhouse) was on his way back to his plantation because he could not get anyone to go back to that barn with him, the people around these parts hate men in our profession. So, when we met, it made me happy. You see boy it was easy to track you down while you were on horseback but then your trail went cool. I see now that you decided to go on foot, very clever, but there is one thing we had in our favor. North is the only direction you people know, and when we ran into Vernon, we knew we were on the right track, and that we would catch up with you later. Vernon hears told me you were traveling with other run-a-ways. Where did they go?"

I told him the truth I said, "in another direction."

"In which direction," said the leader.

Paul responded by saying, "Like you said we only know one direction and that is North."

The leader looks at me and smile, then he said, "my, my, my you do have a very big mouth on you boy."

Then he said in a loud voice, "GET HIM!"

All five men rush me at the same time. I wrap my arm around the first man head and squeezed as hard as I could until I heard something pop. I let go and he fell to the ground dead. I was holding my own until the leader hit me on the back of my head. I fell to my knees, the other four men grabbed me and put me on my back. The leader said, "It is going to be easy to bring you back, do you know why boy, because Niger you are wanted dead or alive. And I pick dead."

He raised his hammer above his head and froze.

At first his men were looking at me grinning, and when nothing happens, they look at their leader wondering what is taking so long to hit me. That is when they notice an arrow in his head. The man beside him had a funny look on his face. His head has a star in his eye. The other men stood up to see where it came from. Hell, I wonder myself.

Two men and a woman stepped out of the woods. The woman was wearing a black robe that covered everything but her eyes. One of the remaining slave hunters said, "who are you?"

The person in black said, "The last person you will ever see."

One of the men said, "kill them, kill them all, and we will have our way with the wench, and we will bring this other nig…"

Before he could finish what, he was going to say, an arrow went in his mouth and out the back of his head.

The other men died just as quickly too. The women had move so fast that the others died where they stood.

The two men and the woman walk toward Paul, I was still amazed at what just happen, that is when Scott extended his hand and ask me to join the group, "you don't have to worry about men like them ever again," and that is when I became the fourth member of The-Five.

At the campfire party. The fire was still burning high when Scott spoke to Paul, "You have come a long way since then my friend." John said, "If those same six men attached you today, you would be able to handle them by yourself."

Michelle asks, "what ever happened to the other run-a-way slaves, or do you know?"

Paul said, "I do not know what happened to Harriet, but the others have a Tavern here in the camp. It is funny because they made it heard before I did. But that is another story only they can tell.

Susan looked at Paul and said, "you are truly a great man my king. My heart beats for you."

John's Story

JOHN'S TABLE OF CONTENTS

John's Story

Sandy turned to John and said, "We have heard from everyone except you. Please tell us your story but wait I must get some more food and drinks before you start."

The others got up to do the same. When everyone came back with their food, drink, pillows, and blankets. Everyone sat around to listen to what John had to say. People sat on stools, chairs, boulders, they sat on the ground with blankets wrapped around them with their food and drinks in hand ready to listen to John.

Paul smiles at all the attention John is getting.

Paul said to Scott, "John is loving this."

Scott, Mark, and Sylvia all agree with Paul. Sandy said, "Okay John, we all are ready."

"Yes, John I can't wait to hear this." Said Paul.

John had his head down to get his thoughts together. When he raised his head, everyone saw something they rarely seen, the look on John face. He was focused. The only time he has that look, is when he is about to go into battle.

John started his story by saying. "My family is very wealthy. We had land, livestock, and we own a blacksmith shop in town where my father and I spent our time making weapons. Not for anyone special, it was just a hobby.

My two older brothers Jordan and Matthew, Jordan is the oldest and Matthew who is very smart. They work on our farm and were incredibly good at it. My brothers enjoyed farming. We had a large field of corn which we sold in town, along with our cattle. We make a good living from that alone. That is until the British came. They wanted all our crops, and half of our stock to be sent back to England in the name of their king.

Now do not get me wrong the British was willing to pay for what they took. But what they were offering was a small amount.

My father and I were in town at the time when the British were at our farm. So, what I am telling you is what my mother told us.

My older Brother Jordan refuse payment it was so little for our corn. He threw the money back at the British and told them to leave our land. The officer replied, "you are subject of our king. So, for this land, the crops, and cattle belong to England. The money I gave you is fair. We did not have to give you anything."

Jordan pulls his pistol out, and point it at the officer and said, "Get off our land now."

The officer smile and said, "You are a brave lad." After saying that he mounted his horse and road off.

An hour pass and the officer return with a lot of troops, Jordan and Matthew ran out of the house and stood on the pouch with their muskets. The British officer saw this and told his troops to fire on the house. They miss them.

Before I go any further, I told you we make weapons as a hobby, well my brother and I are also good shots. So, when the British miss, both Jorden and Matthew took aim and fired. Jordan hit and killed the officer, and Matthew killed one of the Sergeants.

Early in our life my father saw how the British started to treat the settlers. So, he decided to take precautions. He built an escape route years ago, a tunnel from the house that led into the nearby woods.

The British return fire and wounded Jordan. My mother came out of the house and help Jordan back in, and into the tunnel, they made a successful escape. The wound that Jordan received was just a flesh wound. My mother and brothers move through the tunnel easily.

They watch from the wood as the British burn down our home and took our crops that my brothers harvest and took all our cattle.

When my father and I came home, we could not believe what we saw.

We lost a lot, our house, our cattle, and our crops. The only thing we have left is the blacksmith shop, and a lot of money that we have saved.

CHAPTER 2

Boom

My brothers were so angry they wanted to join the Army. My father gave them his blessing and wished he could go with them. I wanted to join too, but I was too young.

However, my father said, "I have something special for you." That is when he introduced me to how to make things go BOOM!

He taught me how to make gunpowder, and how to make alcohol blow up. My father told me the correct mixture of the two, to make a massive explosion, Also, he told me how to make wet hay explode into flame, he shown me how to make small explosives that I can throw. He taught me everything he knew about explosives, and how to use them, and I did learn a few things on my own. Like mixing gun powder with small pieces of metal.

After I learned all what my father taught me, I asked him to come with me.

My father said, "no, I can do good for our Army by staying here and making better weapons to aid General Washington. If you find the General, tell him about me.

John paused for a long time, Wanda and Ann touched John on the hand for support.

Wanda and Ann are Daughters of William Bradford. The Five rescue them by doing the raid on William's plantation. Wanda and John fell in love shortly after that. Ann is the youngest sister. The Daughters also have a brother who now works in John's camp.

Wanda said, "If it is too painful Paul you don't have to continue."

John smiled back and said, "It is all right, this is not the first time I reflected on what happened to my home and it still hurts.

I was so angry I wanted to kill every Red Coat I come across. I never did see General Washington, but I did join a group of men from Kentucky and my God, did we kill some Red Coats."

We did not have anyone that can tell us were the Red Coats are located, at first. We did not have any intelligence on were the British forts where, and when ships were coming in, but what we did have was direction on were the war were.

When we came upon people, they were happy to tell us on which way to go, to find the British. So, we track them all day and when we did come upon the British it was evening, they were just starting to make camp, of caused we must do a lot of reconnaissance, but we had to do it at a distance because we did not have the skills to infiltrate a camp. Sometimes we must kill a guard or avoid patrols to get close to the main camp.

I pause my story and say, "Sylvia your skills in getting intel on the enemy is amazing, it makes our job a lot easier." Sylvia nods her head in response.

John continued his story. Like I said we found the British camp. But we needed to know where they have their weapons, and the gunpowder. The British never put the guns, and gunpowder together, it is always in a different wagon. We found the gunpowder by watching them. It was easy to blow that wagon up one go shot and BOOM. We did not see a chow wagon, which made us believe that they were low on food. The British must have a hunting party out. I suggested to leave a few men behind to keep an eye on their camp. The rest of us went to intercept the hunting party.

The hunting party was located on its way to their camp carrying todays kill to feed the troops, we sat up an ambush further down the road, the plan was simple, we wait until the hunting party is in the center of the ambush then we open fire.

We waited until the British arrived. When the right time came, we attacked, afterward, there was no one left alive. We buried the men in separate graves, so they could not be found, we would take the weapons, gunpowder, and food for ourselves.

Because of our small numbers the only way we could engage the British was a lot of hit and run tactics, until our numbers grew enough to stand and fight them head-to-head.

The British realize that the hunting party was not coming back. So, they went looking for them. I could not have planned it any better than this, our plan is to get them to use their weapons, and gunpowder on which they are low. We waited until they became weak from hunger, it will make it easy to engage them. They will be confused, nerves, and irritated. However, the British are a train Army, it is going to take a little bit more to break them.

"So, what is next?" said one of the men.

"Their gunpowder and weapons," said John.

What we need is distraction. I sent Buster (Buster is one of John's loyal followers.) Buster stands, 5ft. 5in. nice build man for his size, not too fat, not to skinny. He is very quick on his feet and ready to do anything that John asked him to. One hundred yards in front of their camp in the woods with a keg of gunpowder he planted near a tall tree. Buster made a fuse from the gunpowder by pouring the power on the ground making a trail from the keg. By doing it this way it gives buster time to get away before the explosion.

When Buster felt he was far enough, he waited for a signal from John.

When everyone got in position, we waited for the Red Coats, this is the hardest part of an ambush, but they did not have to wait long. The British came to a stop in the middle of our trap.

John gave the signal by sounding like a cow.

Buster said to himself, "well here goes nothing." Then he lit the fuse. After, he ran as fast as he could away from the keg the explosion was loud, the British was surprised when the tree falls, across the road. They were caught off guard. I gave the order to fire; we all open fire on them. They tried to return fire but were confused who to fire at. However, we had no problem, we have killed everyone.

The victory over the British was our first, and it felt good. Our next move is to kill the rest of the Red Coats.

The rest of the British retreated back to their Fort, we follow them to see where they were going, we are still too small of a group to attack the fort. So, we must take them out of the protection of the walls or bring the walls down around them. The British are very weak, and are not as alert, they now know that there will be no food tonight. And they are prone to making mistakes. Pulse, when we killed their troops, and hunting party that we spread them thin, and put holes in their defense.

The first day we quietly planted explosives around the walls of the Fort. No one notice us What we were doing. Now, we are ready, I gave the signal by firing a shot in the air so everyone could light the fuse at the same time. The fuse was lit the gunpowder trail burn even and smoothly. The kegs were close together around the wall and went up at the same time, it was a violent BOOM!

This shook up the whole Fort. After the smoke had settled, the only thing standing were the command tents.

Paul interrupted John, "stop all that boom, boom stuff if you are going to tell the story, tell it without the boom. Paul was irritated.

Everyone around the campfire laughed and so did John, but he continued without responding to Paul's comment.

John went on with his story.

We fired at a few soldiers in their camp, we kill half of them before we ran off into the woods. The British started to chase us which brought them pass a buried keg of gunpowder mix with nails. That we planted earlier. When the Bulk of the soldiers was at the keg, one of the rebels that was in a tree fired on the keg. The keg exploded killing and wounded a lot of soldiers. This time we just departed the area leaving the red coats in wonderment. The one is that was a live help the wounded back to what was left of their Fort.

CHAPTER 3

Coward

The British officer that is now in charge of this platoon is Captain Oxford, a very fat man who is fears his own shadow, so, when things started to go wrong. The soldiers look at the Junior officers and sergeants for leadership.

There was one more keg of gunpowder we left behind. When the keg exploded it spread fire about twenty-five yards from the explosion, the captain ran into the command tent, which was on fire, he was so scared he did not notice that the tent was blazing. He was so scared he would not come out.

A lieutenant and two other men went into the tent to drag him out. When the four men came out, it is obvious to see that Captain Oxford was afraid, and his man see it too. The captain looked around and saw everyone staring at him.

"What are you men looking at? Why are you staring at me? Put this fire out," said Captain Oxford."

To hide his embarrassment, he turns to the lieutenant who saved his life and said, "This is all your fault you left the camp unguarded, this will go bad on your records lieutenants," said Captain Oxford.

Another officer step forward and said, "sir we just save your life."

The captain ignored the other officer and said, "And lieutenant, another thing you do not put your hand on me again do you understand."

Bout lieutenant replied, "yes sir."

As the two lieutenants walked away from the captain, one said to the other.

"We should have left his fat ass in there; look, we have to talk; the captain is going to get us all killed before the war is over."

"You're right, we have to get rid of this coward." Said the other lieutenant.

The first lieutenant said surprisingly, "Are you talking about murdering our superior officer? Do you know the consequences for that?"

The second lieutenant said, "We do not have to do anything we will leave that to the rebels."

The two lieutenants walk to their tent that they share before they went inside, when they came out the two sat down at a campfire just outside their tent.

"Tell me something how did our platoon became the laughingstock of the regiment?" said one of the lieutenants.

The first lieutenant said, "it was after the captain arrived. The captain is the nephew of our commanding officer, Colonel Andrew Hayes. Colonel Hayes is trying to give the captain courage by putting him with us, but it backfired. As soon as things started getting rough, he will call a retreat, or will fake being sick so he would not be able to go out on patrol because of him we became the laughingstock of the regiment."

The first lieutenant said, "you know we heard a lot about you before you came here and assigned to our company. We thought things would get better, but they mostly stayed the same."

The other lieutenant said, "because our Captain is a coward and the entire regiment knows that, but no one says anything because of his uncle."

John and his men went back to their camp happy and proud that everything went as plan.

Before John join his men, he put a keg of gunpowder where everyone was setting. Then he put a trial of gunpowder away from the keg.

With a wave of his hand a man lit the trial, just as John sat down with the key member of his men and plot out their next move.

John said, "The British army works like gunpowder. The lit gunpowder trail kept coming closer to the keg, if you do not have a fuse the gunpowder would just sit there, (the fuse kept burring closer). In the British army it is the soldier who are the gunpowder and the officers who is the fuse," (getting closer).

The men started to get nerves some started to run. John moves his foot across the trial of gunpowder just in time to stop the fire before keg exploded, then John said, "If you cut off the fuse the gun powder will just sit there."

John sat back and shared his plan, "So, our next move is to cut off the fuse. We are going to eliminate the officers. We will have to do it when they are on the move, when they are on their way back to their main Fort. We are going to sit a trap here."

John pointed to a place in the sand where he drew a map.

We will put kegs of gunpowder wrapped in chains, to increase the damage. Once the kegs explode, we will fire on the troops doing the chaos.

The British troops was on high alert for the rest of the night, and into the morning. Colonel Hayes sent his nephew platoon out on patrol. After what has happened in the last few days. Captain Oxford tried to pull off an excuse because he could not go. But this time the Colonel would not have it and sent him out anyway. They went out for a day and made camp everyone can see that the captain was scared to the point of losing his mind. After a sleepless night, he was relieved to know that the platoon was about to head back to the fort or what was left of it. Still tense, the British started to break camp. One man was saying, "I'll be glad when we get back to the Fort."

When the British army finished braking camp and started the march back to the Fort everyone is relieved that they would soon be out of danger. The British got to the area where John and his men were waiting. John told his men to stand by. But one man, who is new, was impatient, this man decided to disregard John order and fired before its time.

The round hit the redcoat in front of the march this cause everybody to stop. The kegs went off in front of the British troops and failed to kill the rest of the officers that is when everyone started to shoot at them.

The officers who survived gathered what troops, got them online and returned fire, this forced John to retreat. His men were no match for a well-trained British Armey in a gunfight head-to-head.

John was angry that his plan was not successful, but he did manage to kill their Captain and a lot of the troops before his men where force into the woods.

When John and his men got to their own camp everyone was happy. Except for John.

When everyone gathers around their campfire everybody was happy and was talking among themselves, John walk over to the man who fired the shot that kill the captain and with his fits hit him a long side of his face and knocked him off his feet.

John told him, "You did not follow my orders, and because of that, you will not be going on any missions with me again. When I tell you, to hold your fire, I mean hold your fire. Because of your impatience, you allowed two officers to get the rest of their troops and return fire. When there is a mission, you are to stay behind. You are to clean weapons and make sure the arsenal is secure and just help around the camp."

The man responded, "I thank you got it wrong. I will be going on missions, and who are you to tell me I am not?"

The man's name is Jordan Johnson he stands a good foot tall over John and very muscular and mean looking.

The rest of the men back up, not knowing what to expect.

John quickly bent over and pick up a stick that was halfway in the fire and planted it alongside of Jordan's head.

When Jordan went down John kick him in the head then jump on Jordan's chest and continue beating the man in his face.

John turn to the man who was in charge and said, "I am done, no longer I will be with this unit. You can have this."

Then John picked up his equipment and started to leave. Four other men pick up their equipment and left with him. But Jordan was not done yet, He got to his feet and ran after John.

John turned around just in time to see Jordan coming toward him but, Jordan stops short, he told John. "No man has ever knock me off my feet, you are the first. Want I am trying to say is, I am sorry for not following your orders, you are a good leader, I see that now, you have my utmost respect and loyalty. I am asking you please, allow me to go with you on your journey, remarkable things are about to happen to you, and if you allow me to let me tag along with you. You have my word that nothing like this will happen again."

John looked at Jordan hard in his eyes and saw that Jordan was very sincere in what he was saying. After seeing this, John said to him, "Get your stuff."

I did not leave the group because of Jordan, I left because I felt theirs something bigger waiting for me. What, I do not know but it is out there, and I will find it.

They traveled for a couple of days not saying much, just a little small talk.

But one night when they pitch camp John turn to Jorden and said, "tell me something Jorden, when I look into your eyes a few days ago I saw something that I never seen before do you have vision?"

Jordan answered, "Sometimes I foresee things that had come true, but not all the time, and sometimes I get this gut feeling that I cannot ignore.

I do not know what it is but when I get it something is going to happen."

John said, "that can be very useful."

Nothing else was said. Two guards were posted to keep watch. Everybody ate and bedded down for the night and went to sleep. No one knew what they would be involved in tomorrow.

The next day John and his men broke camp, they pick a direction and went that way. After walking miles, they heard a lot of people talking about British troops, after investigating they found a large group of British soldiers nearby, this is what John was waiting for.

John wonders why they did not come upon any patrols, well that is something to thank about later. They have not sent one out yet.

John seized the opportunity to do something to cause Havoc, he had his men positioned their self around the regiment and gave them each five wooden balls with a fuse.

Jordan asks John, "What is this?"

John replied, "I call them my little balls of destruction. The wooden balls are filled with gunpowder, nails, and glass, you light the fuse and throw them at the British."

Unknowing to John there was someone else there who had plans to attack the British.

Scott and his Marines were there in hiding. Scott has already positioned his men right behind John's men. Scott gave the word to hold back to see what these men are about to do.

CHAPTER 4

The Introductions

Just before Scott gave the orders to attack. John and his men started to throw their balls of destruction at the British, the balls blowup everywhere. Blast, after blast, after blast. A lot of red coats died and was injured, and something they did not count on. The British was confused, they did not know where the blast was coming from.

This is when Scott saw the opportunity and gave the order. "Attack!" Scott's men open fire from all direction which cause more confusion.

John was surprised at the number of men around him. He was unaware of all the men that was hidden. He had no idea, no clue, that Scott and his men was in the area. How could he have known that; they were all hiding.

John has an opportunity to see Scott's men in action and was very empress. Thanking to himself this is the group of people I been looking to join. They are highly organized. Their strategy is outstanding they are placed around the British regiment in a way that the British would not know what directions the shorts are coming from.

John must know the head man in charge of these men, he will ask permission to join his crew. John did not have to wait long.

After the chaos, Scott took people hostage. Among them were the two lieutenants who got away from John a few days ago.

While the colonials were still wrapping up things. John and his few men were strolling through the camp and came upon the prisoners. John saw the two lieutenants from earlier and could not help thinking how close he came killing them. The lieutenants never knew who John was. John and his man continue walking they came to an area where they decide to sit down and recap everything that went on.

John was talking to his men in how they contribute to the downfall of the British regiment. He informs them how proud he is of them.

John and his men notice the people walking pass were smiling at them, even tip their hats.

As John finished his briefing his man on what took place today, a very hug Black man with a big, hammer walks toward them, he stops at the place were John and his men was sitting, the hug man said, "Who speaks for this group"

John stood up and said, "that would be me."

The hug guy said, "you and your man saved a lot of lives today, Scott wants to speak to you."

"Who is Scott?" John said.

"Scott is the one who organized this assault on this regiment, come with me." Said the big man.

We started walking toward a large tent. I assume that Scott was inside, I did not say anything to the big guy with the big hammer, he seemed that he does not talk much, I just follow his directions.

As we entered the tent it was not hard to pick out Scott, you can see the confidence overflowing, there were some colonels in the back of him, listening to him, taking orders from this Scott.

The man with the hammer introduces us to him, the hug guy said, "these men are the one's responsible for the explosives."

John held his hand out to shake Scott's hand and said, "My name is John."

Scott took his hand and said, "my name is Scott Martin, I want to thank you for all the lives you have save today, but tell me how you knew that we were here to attack that regiment?"

John looked at Scott in wonderment and said, "I had no idea you were there. We saw the regiment and we decide to kill some redcoats. We had planned to throw a few bombs and then run. It is a tactic that I have used before, a kind of harassment every time we see them. We kill a few more, then we take off."

Scott said, "that is a brilliant strategy for a small band of people, you can have them chasing you for days, all the while depleting their numbers with your bombs. Until the British run into a larger army. Is there a large army you relate to?"

Scott looked at the man called John hard, he already knew the answer to that question, because his unit is the only one in the area. If John answers yes, Scott will know something is wrong.

John said, "no it's just us, we harass the redcoats as much as we can until they get too close to us then we will abandon everything and make our get-a-way."

Scott smile and then said, "in that case John, would you like to be a part of a bigger unit?" I can really use a man like you and your skills."

John looked back at all his men, they were shaking their head up and down to show John that they are all in with what Scott is offering. John turn back to Scott and said, "We will be honored sir."

Scott smiled knowing that this was the missing part to what he was trying to form.

Scott said to John, "there are a few other people you should know. You have already met Paul; he is the one with the big hammer. Mark is a man you will know later he is on a mission; you will meet him when he gets back. Sylvia will introduce herself later. In the meantime, get yourself something to eat and rest. We are going to wait until Mark gets back before we go on our next plan of attack.

Scott turned and pointed to a Sergeant in the room. This Sergeant will show you to a supply wagon, get a tent to house you and your man for the time being.

"Thank you, sir." Said John.

John and his men followed the Sergeant out and toward the supply wagon. We found a tent large enough to house all five of us comfortably, we began to talk among ourselves. One of John's men lean forward and said, "It is good to have a roof over our head for a change."

Another man said, "yell, but I prefer the stars."

A third man said, "I don't know about you men, I am happy to be here."

Then the first man notice movement inside the tent, "What the hell," he said.

When John and the rest of the men turn around it was too late to react,

Six people all dressed in black with a sword held at their throats. John had no place to go, he could not move nor his men.

Now that John and his men are secured, a sixth person walked toward John, the person took off her hood. They all were surprised to see that it was a woman she said, "My husband told you that you will be meeting me later. My name is Sylvia Martin, welcome, you have empress me with what you have done today and that is not easy to do. As time goes on you will know more about me and my people. Until then. We just stop by to say hello." The ninjas relax and take a step back from John's men.

Everyone's attention was on Sylvia, when they noticed the other people that were there were gone. Someone asks,

"How did she get in here without us knowing?" said one man.

John turned back to ask Sylvia that very question, and she was gone.

"Where did Sylvia go, and how did she get out?" Said John.

Everyone stood up and looked around in bewilderment.

"Have they been in here all along," said another.

"No, they couldn't have, we are the ones that put up the tent." John said.

Then there was silence.

John said, "I am going to enjoy being with these people."

Everyone agreed, they decided to go to sleep for the night to be ready for whatever tomorrow will bring.

CHAPTER 5

John Proves Himself

When John woke up the next morning, he noticed that there was an eerie feeling in the air. He stepped outside of the tent, looked around to the other people and noticed that everyone was so serious. Everyone is getting their equipment together; they are making sure the musket is clean and having enough ammo.

John scents that something is going on. So, he decided to talk to Scott to find out what it was. He reached the front of Scott's tent and was stopped by one of the guards.

"Where you thank, you're going?" said the guard.

John answer, "I'm going to see Scott."

"Did the Colonel send for you?" Said the guard.

"No," said John.

Colonel Scott is in a meeting; he will get with you and your men afterward." Said the guard.

John is not used to being left out of planning noir does he like it, and he must wait until things are decided without him, I do not think so. John is the man that usually making the plans. So, he decided that he should be in there with Scott.

John turned to his man and said, "I need you to keep the guard occupy while I get in the tent."

One of the men said, "that will be easy, I'll keep his mine on me." John man walks toward the guard. The guard watches him as he approaches.

When John's man got close enough to the guard, he started to talk to him. The guard was in a very talkative mood. They started to talk about anything, and everything, this gave John the opportunity to sneak by and go inside the tent.

On the way inside John herd Scott say, "We will have to take the fort before we take on the ship."

Then it happened two swords were in John's throat, everyone in the tent turned and saw him.

Scott smiled and said, "let him in."

John became puzzled, where are Scott's Captains, his Lieutenants. He has met Paul, The Big man, with the big hammer, he knew who Scott was, and Sylvia introduced herself to me. But I have not met this tall curly headed Black man on his right looking at the map. Come to think of it, I have not seen anyone in uniform. I see now this is the Colonials Army, and he answers only to General George Washington or did I join some advanced Military unit. These men are train to well to be military. So, why aren't they in uniform, who are these people really?

Scott said, "What took you so long to get here? Come over to the table John and meet our missing member." Scott introduces the two men.

"Mark this is John. He saved a lot of lives a few days ago when you were not here, he might be valuable to our plans." Said Scott.

John, through Scott was referring to the plans he had laid out on the table, but only Scott, Sylvia, Mark, and Paul knew what Scott meant.

Scott brought John up to date in what he was planning, "In three days there is a ship coming in with fresh supplies and troops. We must destroy that ship, but before we do that, we must take down this fort," said Scott.

John asked, "why can't we just bypass the fort and address the ship?"

Scott replied, "if we do that, we'll have the British at our backs as well in our front we will not be able to survive that."

John said, "How are you going to pull this off, by taking the fort. A frontal attack would be suicide.

"Scott replied, "We are planning to send a group of people inside to eliminate as many people as possible so our attack will be swift and easy and fewer casualties.

John pause for a few second and said, "there may be a better way Scott, you do not have to send a lot of men inside. Let me and my men go inside and put some explosives in some key places around the Fort. A Fort like this is big, the British have patrols inside checking things like doors, the armory, and other buildings, they will check the gunpowder, ammunition, and after each check they have a signal that everything is okay. If the signal is not sent or received the alarm will sound. Scott, Sylvia, Paul, and Mark agree. So, it was decided that John and his men will go in and sat some explosives, then we will be able to take the fort with little casualties.

"Give me an hour, I'll come up with something that will meet your approval." Said John.

Scott turned to the other members and said, "Let us step outside and leave him with his thoughts, John, we will see you in one hour. If you have any questions, we will be getting something to eat. The Sergeant will let you know where we are."

The moment Scott stepped outside Paul said to Scott, "Well it works just like you said, how did you know that he was going to suggest looking at the maps?"

Scott smile and said, "The man has a good head on his shoulders. Besides if you notice when I show him the plans, I did not mention anything about explosives, that part he will put in. I thank he is the final piece of our puzzle to the making of the five."

Mark intervenes, "Well let's see how he'll handle the fort, and the ships before we come to that conclusion."

Paul nods his head in agreement and said, "let's get something to eat."

Paul and Mark walk away talking to each other.

Scott notice Sylvia staring at the tent. Scott said, "You haven't said nothing at all, what is your take on all of this?"

Sylvia replied, "this John, he will make us very strong Martin, and of course I will go along with anything you say anyway."

Scott put his arm around her and said, "Sweetheart, let's get something to eat."

It did not take John an hour to know what had to be done. He looked at the plan and knew right away that the walls had to come down. But, before that, his men will have to sneak in the Fort somehow and plant explosives in key places, the mess tent, the barracks, and the Armory must go. BOOM!

When the attack starts, they are going to assemble their forces. John pointed at the map, right here in the middle of the square to prepare for a counterattack. John will blow their formation apart, during the confusion that's when Scott's people can come in and take the fort.

After John finished with his planning, he joins Scott, Sylvia, Paul, and Mark for something to eat. John sat down with them and told everyone, "I thank you are going to like what I have planned, but I'm going to need some help with it, the only way it can work, I have to get inside."

Scott said, "Okay eat up, then we'll see what you got."

Nothing was said on the way back to the command tent until everyone was inside. That is when John laid out his plan.

After Scott pause for a second then he said, "yes, yes, this will work, and as for you getting inside, that will fall under Sylvia, she can get you inside."

John look at Sylvia and remember how she got in and out of their tent the day before, he said, "yes I believed she can."

Then Scott laid out the whole plan. Scott turned to the group and said, "Okay, this is how it is going to go down. Sylva, you take John, his men, and most of your people, or how many you thank you may need.

Mark goes along with her. Station your men in various places in the Fort where they can see everything. Sylvia, once you get your people inside put them around the square, after John blows the square, have the ninjas attack, drive them into the barracks."

Scott turned to John and said, "I want you to place your explosives alone the wall of the fort, before you go in, place them hear, hear, and there."

That is when I realized that my plan was not to show Scott how to take the Fort it was to add to Scott's plan.

Scott looks at everyone and said, "Choose your people well, tell them to get some rest because it's going to be a very interesting night."

Scott looked at Paul and said, "Paul you and I will make ready the main force. As soon as the wall comes down, we will move. I want three sharp shooters to shoot and blow kegs of gunpowder against the wall. Okay everyone, any questions?"

John took this opportunity to ask the questions that he always wanted to ask ever since he came to the group.

John asks Scott, "There's something I want to ask you."

Scott smile and said, "I know that you are confused."

"Yes I am.," said John.

Scott stops everything he was doing and said to John smiling, "ask your questions."

John asks, "who are you people really? You are not an army of the colonies, and I know damn well you are not the Military, so, who are you people? You even have a couple of Black man acting as your Captains."

"Their ranks are Major. Said Scott.

Then John put up his hands in front of Scott, palms out and continued with his question.

"Now don't get me wrong, I don't have anything against Black people, but you have to admit this is kind of unusual, and a woman." John paused.

Then he started again, "Well after she introduce herself to me, I can see why she will be here."

Scott answered, "how good of you to notice. I will explain everything and more after the mission."

John reply, "after we take the Fort?"

Scott answer, "the ship"

After Scott and I had our little talk, I join my men, and we settle down, relaxing until the sun went down.

Later when it was starting to get dark.

Scott called everybody together and told us to get prepared, we got our weapons and things we needed for explosives. My men were ready they knew what to do, we need to put three kegs of gunpowder in front of the Fort. One on each side of the gate and the other ten yards to the right of it. Some of my men are to join me on the right side of the Fort. Ms. Sylvia was dressed in black; so, where she goes, the followers will get us inside easily.

When darkness came, the British sent out its first patrol. Scott instructed us to avoid the patrol and let them thank that everything is peaceful.

The first patrol came back to the Fort satisfied that everything was all clear.

It was very dark when the British sent out their second patrol. The sky was thick with clouds that covered the moon light. This is what Scott was waiting for, he gave the nod to Paul and Mark.

Paul, Mark, and their men waited until the Patrol reach their farthest point from the Fort, and then they attack. It was quick and easy. Because of the distance from the Fort, the British did not here the gunshots. Mark and his men with their long bow, shot the officer and their Sergeants. Then Paul and his man killed or captured the rest of the patrol with their muskets. The word is dispatched to Scott, phase one is completed. On to phase two.

Everyone was in position they went over the plan several times in their head, down to the men. Everybody knows exactly what they are supposed to do. We were all waiting for the signal from Scott.

Scott received the report from Paul and Mark. Then he signals Sylvia to begin phase 2.

Sylvia and her ninjas immediately went to work, up and over the wall without a sound. They killed all the centuries and the inside patrols.

Anyone who steps out of a building or tent met with a ninja and its blade, the ninja secured the Fort phase 2 is complete. The signal has been given to Scott that the Fort is secured. Start phase 3.

Scott received the signal as plan, then he nodded to start phase 3. Scott looked at John and said, "Go!"

John's men went to the gate and place their kegs of gunpowder on each side of the gats and ten yards to the right of it just like they were instructed. After placing the kegs. John and his men join Sylvia and her ninjas.

The ninjas were there to help John and his men to get inside. Once inside his men reach the top of the wall, they look down into the compound of the Fort. It was eerie, in the compound it appeared to be shadows moving all over the place.

John along with his men made it to the British armory and took what gunpowder they need.

The gunpowder was placed throughout the Fort.

At first John was going to Blow up the armory but decided that we can use these guns and extra gunpowder.

John fixed a special keg, a mixture of gunpowder and nails for fragmentation, then he buried the keg halfway in the middle of the courtyard. Where the formation will take place.

After the explosive were in place and the men were in positions Sylvia gave the order to John. John lit the fuse that was leading toward the gunpowder at the building where troops ate and the food was stored, then he lit the fuse to the keg of gunpowder to the command building, which is when everything started to get interesting. BOOM! The sound of the explosion wakens everyone, but before the British had a chance to react the other keg exploded, BOOM! Went to the command center. The commanding officer and both aids died in the explosion.

A couple of officers were looking for the commanding officer. Once they realize that he is not coming, they turn to see who was in charge.

Confused about the chain of command, he heard someone yelling orders. "Get the men in formation to return fire." Other Captain's was barking out orders.

In the meantime, Scott gave the signal to his Marines, they took aim and squeezed the trigger, three men, three muskets, and each man fired, all three-round hit their mark. The front of the Fort went up in one big fireball.

The remaining officers saw the front of the Fort disappeared and in the middle of all the chaos a lieutenant try to maintain order, he form his men in formation to repel what is about to come through the hole where the gate used to be. The Lieutenant finally got his men together and was ready to return fire on anybody that comes though that hole in the wall.

Sylvia was about to order her people to attack when John stopped her. She looked at John wondering why.

John said nothing, he just took careful aim with his musket, he squeezes the trigger, and the round hit the keg that was half buried in the middle of the British formation. Boom! Lot of the British was either killed or wounded.

John smiled, he turned to Sylvia and nodded his head. Sylvia smiled back, and then gave the order to attack.

A brief time later, Paul and Scott led their men through the hole in the wall. To their surprise the whole thing was over. The British had surrender.

Paul and Scott were looking around the Fort in amazement thinking to themselves how this can be over so fast, Sylvia walk toward Scott and said, "John, Mark, and I has done the work, you two can do the cleanup while Mark, John, and I start the celebration, after you have finish, you two can join us." Sylvia smiled and walked away toward their camp.

Scott looks at her and said, "yes ma'am."

Sylvia stopped and turned toward Scott and said, "Scott, John is the missing piece to complete The-Five.

Then Sylvia sent for Mark and John to meet her back at the camp immediately.

Paul just looks around and said, "What the hell happen here?"

After the cleanup Scott sent the prisoners to General Washington then he and Paul made their way back to the camp.

Scott told everyone, "This celebration will be brief we have to make plans about the ship coming in."

Later everyone sat down at a table in Scotts commend tent, John was invited to plan their next part, the ship.

Scott addresses the group, "Okay here is what we know, the ship is due in tomorrow with fresh troops and supplies, if we want to make this work, we must stop those troops before they get to shore. So, here is what I propose. We are going to align our Marines along the shore there is where we will engage the British while they are still in their long boats. As they come to shore, Sylvia, and her people will engage them in close combat and this should make things easy.

John said, "If you give me five men you wouldn't have to worry about engaging any troops, we can take the ship out before a shot is fired"

This time when John made a comment about the plan Scott was puzzle,

"And how are you going to do that," said Scott.

John replied, "if you give me five men, we can sneak aboard that ship and blow it out of the water before anyone knows what happen."

Scott said, "If you can do that, you will save a lot of my men lives, but in the meantime in case something goes wrong. We are going to be ready at the shore to prepare for the worst.

At the camp John stood up and said, "you all knew what happened to the ship it went Boom! And that is when I became officially the last number of The Five.

Michelle said, "that was five amazing stories."

Everyone applauded and toasted the five, and when the laughter and the celebration settled down, three African men came to Scott and said, "it is time."

Scott gave them a hard look, knowing exactly what they were talking about.

Scott said, "all of you what to go back, or just you three?" One of the men said, "Us three and more."

Scott looked over to Captain Jeff and said, "The Monika sails in three weeks for Africa, prepare the fleet.

There is more to this story, you will find in the third book of The Five Titled—To the Mother Land.

I hope you enjoy The Five series. Keep on the lookout for more of The Five to come.

TO THE FIVE

www.ingramcontent.com/pod-product-compliance
Lightning Source LLC
Chambersburg PA
CBHW032034310726
48972CB00002B/666